The Sec

by Emn

To all my family and the horses in my life.

Chapter 1

The car was filled with the blue light of morning as they drove across the moors. They had been driving for hours overnight, but Jessie had not been able to sleep. Her brother and sister slept soundly, waking only occasionally as the car bumped in a pothole or to murmur:

"How much longer till we get there?"

The car windows were steamed up and Jessie drew pictures on the foggy glass with a fingertip - smiley faces, sad faces, stars, flowers. She rubbed them all out with a sweep of her hand and through the wet blur she could see ponies, dozens of ponies of all colours roaming across the moorland. She pressed her face up against the window and watched them, as they nibbled at the stunted trees and trotted over the springy turf.

"Can we stop for a minute, Dad?"

Her dad's eyes watched her in the rear view mirror, then glanced at the clock on the dashboard. It had been four hours since their last stop and would be another one at least until they got there.

"Yeah, okay. Just for ten minutes though then we must get on." He pulled over in a lay-by and as soon as he had turned off the engine, Jessie flung open the door and leapt out, like a racehorse released from the starting box.

"No running off!" Jessie's mum called but she was already bounding across the grass, gangly legs

~ 4 ~

leaping over boulders, until she flopped down behind a gorse bush. The yellow flowers smelled of coconut and the damp grass felt cool against her bare legs. The sky was a deep blue and the sun was just beginning to warm the air; it was going to be a hot summer's day. Jessie pressed her fingers into the dew-soaked turf and watched as the ponies wandered around her.

They did not take much notice of Jessie apart from the occasional ear which flicked in her direction. Instead they continued to graze, noisily chewing and snuffling around in the short vegetation. Their breath created misty clouds as it met the cool air and they flicked their long tails.

One piebald pony, its short, fuzzy tail and large curious eyes showed that it was no more than a year old, looked up from where it was scratching against a tree and walked a few steps towards Jessie. It nodded its head up and down and moved a few steps closer. Jessie was so tempted to walk over to it but knew that it would just trot away; she stayed still as curiosity got the better of it. It stretched out its nose and breathed deeply, then in a moment, it had turned around and ambled back to the rest of the herd.

Jessie, too, stood up and ran back to her parents. Her dad was walking through the clumps of bracken with a mug of tea in one hand and half a sandwich in the other. Her mum sat in the car with her legs stretched out of the open door; she was rummaging around in a bag on the back seat, handing a bag of crisps to Jessie's brother, Matthew, who was still sleepily rubbing his eyes. Her little sister, Megan, still slept soundly.

That summer had been the beginning and the end. It was now a year on; Jessie could look back and remember it as a blur of sandcastles, ice creams, arguments and catching crabs off the pier - a summer of sea gulls, fairgrounds, wet towels and slammed car doors; an odd mix of the best and the worst of times, tears soaking into the pillow and laughter across the waves. Now, a year on, Jessie was a little older, a little tougher and a little wiser. A new adventure was just around the corner, one that would change her life in all ways... an adventure that she was both excited and scared to begin.

***

The second time they had driven across that same stretch of moorland they had been one person less and a lot of luggage more. They sat in the hired van, all their possessions hurriedly packed into cardboard boxes and bin bags, and drove away from it all. Jessie's mum, a fake smile painted on her face with lipstick, gripped the steering wheel with white fingers and Jessie rested her head against the window.

It was night and the sky was so clear that haloes of stars framed Jessie's reflection in the glass. She had never been able to sleep in cars, but instead listened to the soft breathing and murmurs of her sleeping brother and sister in the back.

She had thought of one thing only on the journey down. The same words repeated themselves endlessly. The same shouts, slams and shattering glass thudded inside her skull and made her head ache.

Don't do this. Please. Don't take my children away from me.

The last sounds: the scattering gravel, the slam of car doors and the screech of tyres - the sound of Jessie's heart breaking in her chest.

She had not said a word to her mother since. The hours had passed by under the blur of motorway lights, the cats eyes leading the way to some uncertain future. The brief stop at the service station with a dash under fluorescent lighting, where the grey-faced night shift worker continued to sleepily mop the toilet floor. The gulps of hot, sugary tea and then, off again. Back to the black road and the car where condensation dripped down the windows.

Jessie leaned against the glass but her eyes remained wide open the whole way. She watched the sky beginning to lighten. Black to dark blue. The silhouettes of trees appeared and clouds and a few black rooks that burst from tree to sky. The clouds changing. Grey to pink to gold. Houses becoming visible, telegraph wires and back gardens. She imagined she was riding a great black stallion; galloping along endless roads, she clung onto the reins as he bolted, out of control.

When the sky was the pale blue of early morning, the car finally pulled up alongside a cottage.

Its white painted walls stained the blue of the forget-me-nots which grew wildly in the flower beds. The uncurtained windows gaped black like staring eyes, the driveway of cracked flagstones like crazy teeth.

Jessie climbed out of the car and stared at the strange place. It felt a little spooky and unsettling. And yet, the air smelt so familiar. The salt and earth. It reminded her of all those family holidays, of crawling out of the tent and taking a deep breath of clean, fresh air. Her mum fumbled around in her pockets to find a silver key with a tag tied on with string.

"Get it opened up, Jess," she said, handing the key to Jessie "I'll wake the other two."

***

The unsettling feeling remained as Jessie explored the rooms, enjoying the early moments when she was the only one inside the house. She could still feel the house's previous occupants lingering in the shadows and watching her from the beams of dusty sunlight that filtered through the windows. She walked down the hallway with its cold, tiled floor and coat hooks above the radiator. She blew cobwebs from the taps at the kitchen sink and drew circles around the stains on the worktops. In the sitting room, Jessie tried to imagine a roaring fire crackling in the grate, but it was empty and a draught rattled in the chimney. She ran her fingers through the thick layer of dust on the doorframe and felt her chest aching at the loneliness of this place.

Jessie's mum came through the doorway, arms loaded with bags and she threw open a window to let the fresh air in.

"Have you found your room yet, Jess?" she asked, leading her up the stairs into a bedroom.

The room was small with a low ceiling which sloped down to a window. There was a deep alcove which created a dark, shadowy corner and Jessie shuddered when she saw a spider scuttle away as the door opened with a creak.

"It'll need a good clean but once all your stuff's in it'll feel more like home."

Jessie walked over to the window. The thick stone walls made a ledge around it and there was a wooden sill which was wide enough to sit on. She pulled herself up and sat with her arms wrapped around her legs, looking out of the window. Outside, she could see a small garden with a low brick wall and beyond that, moorland stretched out to the horizon. Jessie peered out moodily from behind her fringe, but her gaze was caught by something moving on the hills.

A band of bay ponies grazed at the scrubby grass. There were seven of them. One walked a little ahead of the others. Two had stopped grazing to groom each other, big teeth scratching at withers. The rest ambled slowly on, moving like one creature, understanding each other so completely that they seemed to know what they were all thinking, even without words. Jessie wished that humans could do without words too.

"I know you hate me at the moment, Jess, but it had to be done. We couldn't go on the way we were."

"I KNOW," Jessie said loudly. Without words, Jessie had only thoughts. Images of her father in their old home, alone.

"I know you miss your Dad." Jessie tucked her face into her knees. "But you'll still see him and you'll settle in here in time."

Jessie pictured him, slumped on the sofa. Crying over the kitchen sink. Hurling mugs and vases and photo frames to the floor.

"I don't care about him. I don't care about you. Just leave me alone." Jessie's mum walked over to her and stroked her hair.

Jessie thought of him waking up, red-eyed and straightening the same clothes he had been wearing when they left - what clothes had he been wearing? Jessie felt that she was forgetting him already.

"Be angry with me for a while. I don't blame you. Just not for too long, eh?" She turned around and went back to unloading the car. Jessie thought of her dad, alone, making breakfast. The only sound in that silent house was that of the knife spreading marmalade on toast.

***

As the hours ticked by on the old kitchen clock that Jessie wished had been left behind, the house was slowly filled with all the familiar things. It felt wrong to see them in a new setting: the lamp that was now on a dusty shelf should have been by the window, the picture of a boat should be back on the wall of her father's office and the photograph of her family should have been above the mantelpiece, not tucked behind a vase as it was now.

She caught a reflection of her mum in the bathroom mirror, dabbing at her eyes with toilet roll. Her brother sat in front of the TV, the first thing he had made them unpack, his eyes glazed over in the dusty light. Megan slept soundly in her cot, unaware of anything that had happened today. Jessie wished she could be like her.

She went outside. She walked to the end of the garden and a desire to just keep on walking overcame her. Over the wall, Jessie scrambled, bits of stone and moss flaking away under her fingers, and she was out in the open moorland. She kept walking, climbing higher up over the rocks, stumbling on the loose shale and tripping on the tussocks of spiky grass. Her fingers tightened in her pockets and she could feel her heart hammering against her ribs.

Anger bubbled up inside her: anger at her mum for taking them away; anger at her brother and sister for sleeping through it; anger at herself for allowing it all to happen.

The salty breeze tangled Jessie's dark hair. The earth beneath her seemed to throb and shudder through her body with every gulping breath she struggled to take. Her jaw felt tense and she could feel tears welling in her eyes.

Amidst the vast openness of the moors, Jessie felt like a wild animal. She felt as though she was one of the moorland ponies, with the prickle of gorse against her legs and the roar of the sea in her ears. She stood up, tried to escape these strange feelings, and kicked violently at a few stones that bounced their way to the bottom of the tor.

Jessie clutched her stomach and screamed at the top of her voice. The sound carried away on the breeze and the ponies looked up at her. She screamed again and thought of her mum looking up from behind a pile of cardboard boxes. She screamed a third time and she thought of her dad pausing and listening as he picked up pieces of shattered photo frame.

Silence. For a few moments there was silence - no sound from the sea, from the gulls or the whispering breeze... and then, as if an answer, a piercing whinny echoed amongst the rocks. A neigh that was so shrill and panic stricken that it made all other thoughts vanish from Jessie's mind. A creature that was so full of terror that Jessie knew she must find it. She scrambled down as quickly as her legs could carry her.

She wound her way around the tor and headed in the direction that the noise had come from. Nestled amongst the bracken, only metres from the cliff edge, a small grey house and cluster of outbuildings looked out to sea. There was a footpath that led through some bushes and low trees and Jessie could not stop herself following it.

The footpath opened out into a paddock that was more weeds and bare patches than grass. Jessie knew that she should not be here, she knew she should not trespass, but the desire to see the horse that she was sure must be here was too strong. The buildings were very run down, brambles tangled through smashed window panes and rusting farm machinery lay in a heap in the corner of a concrete yard.

Jessie peered around, but there did not seem to be anybody about. It was so quiet, only the sound of leaves rustling in the trees and the occasional squawk of a seagull overhead broke the silence. Ivy dangled down from the roof of one white barn, paint peeling on the bottom half of a stable door, Jessie walked over. The stable door was bolted in place and a weaving grill was fastened. A sickly-sweet, rotting smell came over the door as Jessie stood on tip toes to look over. In the dark gloom, she could just see a white shape at the back of the box. It was standing still but as Jessie's eyes adjusted to the lack of light she could see it was a horse.

"Hey," she said softly, "it's okay, come here."

Suddenly, with a crash against the metal grill, the horse lunged against the door. Jessie leapt back, all she saw was a blur of bared teeth, flattened ears, wild eyes and a streak of red blood against white hair.

"GET OUT!" a loud voice shouted from the barn, "GO AWAY AND DON'T COME BACK!"

Chapter 2

Jessie froze. She was caught between the horse, who was still frantically thrashing against the stable door and an angry man slowly making his way towards her.

"Come here, girl!" he shouted.

The sun was setting behind him and his dark silhouette was just a faceless shape, that came slowly closer. In the skies above, a flock of jackdaws chattered noisily as they sped away overhead. The white horse crashed about inside the stable, occasionally lunging towards Jessie with a wild-eyed look of terror on its sunken face. As the man shuffled from side to side, the sun's rays came through in brief flashes of intense yellow, like a camera flash: Jessie felt as though she were frozen in time, unable to escape the photographer's lens.

"Get away from my horse," he moaned, swaying from side to side.

Flashes of light.

Closer and closer.

A red sky and the sweat-slick neck of the white horse; he snapped, teeth gnashing, eyes bulging, over the stable door. The heavy smell of iron and ammonia that came in waves on the too-hot summer air.

A few steps closer and a few steps closer and reality was revealed. The sun streamed freely through the gap between the buildings and the man appeared as he really was. The jackdaws quietened. The horse stood trembling at the back of the box. Jessie could make out the elderly features on the old man's lined face and his blue eyes were watery. He felt more human now - vulnerable. He seemed like someone's granddad - like her own granddad. Where was he now? With an arm wrapped around her father's shoulders, letting him sob into his shirt?

Jessie ran. She slipped through the gate and ran as fast as she could through the dusty paddock, never once looking back. All Jessie thought of as she ran over bracken, over heather, was the horse. She remembered his wild, frightened eyes and the bloody streak across his white muzzle. She remembered his answering call during her moment of utter loneliness. That must have meant something, surely.

Jessie ran along the trampled path across the moors. The sun was setting just above the sea, turning the sky all shades of pinks and purple, its fiery rays shining on the still water. It was like a painting, a canvas across which Jessie was running, her long, dark shadow a black smudge on this multicoloured world. Gulls wheeled in the still air and, looking out to sea, Jessie could imagine all of the strange and beautiful dream-like creatures who danced and swam and tossed themselves amongst the waves. She had never felt this way before, frightened and excited and sad and ecstatic all at once.

The wild ponies, who Jessie had seen through her bedroom window, watched her as she ran on. One or two closest to her, trotted quickly back to the safety of the herd as Jessie dashed past, a flash of white trainers and tangled hair, as she made her way back to the cottage.

The cottage looked different now. The sunset had painted it pink and just this changing light gave it the soft feeling of a fairytale cottage. A warm, cosy place where rabbits cuddled up at nighttimes. A grandmother's house full of memories. Yet, as Jessie drew nearer, she remembered her family inside; remembered the night before and the shouts, screams and slamming doors. The magic vanished.

Jessie peered in through the door. In the past she would have been greeted by angry words and frantic, worried hugs - but the house was silent. Matthew still watched the television. Megan had woken up and gurgled to herself as the dying light filtered through the bars in her cot.

"Where's Mum?" Jessie asked Matthew who only shrugged his shoulders.

She went upstairs and found her mum curled up on the mattress in her bedroom. Black mascara ran down her face and she sobbed quietly into a pillow. She stopped when she saw Jessie in the doorway and tried to wipe her eyes, smearing the black makeup even more.

"Jessie. Please. Come here a minute."

Jessie stayed still.

"Please." Her mum struggled to sit up. Her hair was matted and untidy and her hands reached out to Jessie.

"No."

Jessie felt tears running down her face as she ran into her bedroom and slammed the door. She left bare footprints on the dusty floorboards and the curtain-less windows showed a gaping hole of darkening sky. Although she couldn't see them, Jessie could still sense the ponies out on the moor. Seven dark shapes under the pale moon. She imagined them huddled together, resting. She felt as though they were watching her through the window, seeing her black silhouette against the yellow light of her bedroom.

She lay down and closed her eyes and in the blackness all she saw was the white horse. Alone, in his dark stable. His stained coat a ghostly white. She knew she must go back there again, to find some way of helping him.

***

The following days came and went. Furniture was moved into place and houseplants brightened up window sills. Photographs and books made the cottage feel more homely - but the sheets knotted along the curtain poles and the cardboard boxes still stacked along the walls were a reminder that everything was new and unfinished.

It had only been a few days ago that Jessie had been excitedly looking forward to the school summer holidays, yet now she felt that she would rather be sitting in a classroom with Mrs Thompson at the whiteboard and Clara kicking at the leg of her chair.

"Let's go to the beach!" Jessie's mum exclaimed, attempting to knock the sombre atmosphere out of the house, to make them excited, happy, the children they had been... before. She bundled Megan into a pushchair and closed the computer that Matthew was sitting behind. Jessie flicked her dark hair in front of her eyes, moodily, and followed.

It was the perfect summer day and, down on the hot sand, Jessie could not help but feel a little lighter. For a few moments, she could no longer hear her dad's angry words. The sounds replaced by the squawk of seagulls and lapping waves. The pictures in her head of him slumped over, drunk, on the living room floor swapped for the glitter of the sea and the yellow sand.

As they rounded the far edge of the beach, they passed a cafe. The sound of china clinking and smell of toast and coffee drifted out on the breeze. Inside, on the wooden floor, a terrier lay across his owner's feet as she looked out at the waves. A waiter was laughing with a lady in a loose cotton blouse. An elderly couple, arm in arm, came out of the cafe and climbed slowly down the steps onto the sand.

The man was tall and thin, dressed smartly in a crisp blue shirt and the lady wore a floppy straw hat and had a string of red beads around her neck. Jessie recognised him. It was the man from the other day.

Panic gripped her stomach. They were heading towards each other and were too close to avoid. Jessie kept her head down and walked, half-hidden, by her mum.

"... the ham was pretty good today, wasn't it, Jack? Look at the waves. The gulls... Hello!"

The ladies voice was soft, carried on the summer breeze and Jessie knew the 'Hello' was being addressed to them.

Feeling it rude not to, Jessie looked up and smiled quickly.

"Beautiful day," the lady said.

"Isn't it lovely!" Jessie knew from the way her mum's voice was raised and she chattered excitedly that there was no escaping now.

"We've just moved here. Only a few days ago. And it's one of the most beautiful places... no, no, in fact, it is THE most beautiful place I've ever been to."

Jessie looked up into the old lady's face and recognised the curious smile that had appeared on it.

She had avoided the old man and yet, she could feel his eyes watching her. She could bear it no longer and glanced quickly at him.

He appeared as he had the other evening - a little lost and confused. A look just behind his eyes as though there was something he was struggling to understand. In a moment, he was distracted. His blue eyes spotting a seagull and immediately being drawn up high into the sky, following the bird's soaring flight into the clouds.

Jessie breathed a sigh of relief.

"My name is Helen, and this is my husband, Jack."

"I'm Frances. This is Jessie, Matthew and Megan," her mum gestured to each child in turn.

"Welcome to Polgwiban."

***

Whilst her mum played with her brother and sister, Jessie spent the rest of the day trying to come up with a plan. She saw the grey horse everywhere she looked; he was in the shape of the clouds, on the crest of the waves, in the shadows amongst the dunes. Now that she knew Jack did not recognise her, she felt there must be a way to visit the horse again.

At the first opportunity, when they had got home tired and sandy, and her mum was busy bathing Megan, Jessie slipped out of the house. She left a note on the kitchen table simply saying, *'Gone out - back in a bit'* - and left as she had before, over the garden wall and out across the moors.

She found a better path around the edge of the tor, but it was still rocky and difficult to cross. The journey took about twenty minutes; the whole way there Jessie practised over and over the words that she would say to Helen when she arrived.

Nerves swirled in her stomach and she felt that she might be sick, but she forced herself to remember the horse, to remember why she was doing this. She found the house. It stood all on its own, all the other houses in the area being clustered around the village but this one stood out amongst the cliffs. It's grey walls camouflaged with the granite and the clouds and the sea. Jessie made her way through a low gate and along the garden path. The grass was scorched and brown; a few plants could be seen either sprawling and overgrown or shrivelled and dying.

Jessie knocked on the front door.

"Hello?" Helen opened the door and stood looking puzzled, "I recognise you. The girl on the beach... sorry I don't remember your name."

"Jessie," she replied nervously and she blurted out the speech she had recited on the way over.

"I'm sorry to bother you. Only, I was just wondering if you needed any help with anything. I don't have to start school until after the holidays and I want to try and make a bit of money - help mum out with buying some things for the new house. So I thought I'd ask if people have any jobs. Like dogs to walk? Or a car to wash? Or... anything really."

Helen smiled.

"How old are you, love?" she asked.

"Eleven."

"Eleven? And you trudged all the way out here? Does your mum know where you are?"

Jessie nodded.

"Well. Perhaps you should come in for a minute, I'll get you a drink and I'll have a think if there's anything we need help with."

This felt wrong. Jessie knew that she should never have come here. Her mum would be angry if she knew and she had always told her, over and over again, never talk to strangers. However, she followed Helen inside.

Jessie was ushered to a sofa and a ginger cat immediately leapt up onto her lap where it began purring and kneading at her legs, before settling down for a snooze.

"Would you like some squash, Jessie?" Helen asked from the kitchen.

"Yes. Thank you."

Sitting opposite, on a chair in front of the window, Jack sat quietly watching Jessie. He had that same look in his eyes, as though memories were flitting through his mind like butterflies, that he wasn't quite fast enough to catch hold of.

Suddenly, he gripped the arms of the chair and leant forward.

"I know you," he murmured softly. Jessie felt the nerves begin to slosh about in her tummy again.

"I know you. I know who you are. You're that girl. The one from before," he said, his voice getting louder and more excited.

Helen came rushing through from the kitchen and placed a calming hand on his shoulder.

"I know her. I know that girl."

"Yes, sweetheart, it's the girl from before, the girl on the beach."

"No, no, no. Not from there. I know her from before."

Jessie tried to shake her head but he seemed to have caught one of those butterflies and there was no way he was letting it go.

"Before? When?"

"I know her... it's Anna," he said finally and slumped back in his chair.

"Anna? No, no, it's not Anna." Helen dashed to a chest of drawers and began rummaging around.

"Anna would be much older now. She'd be all grown up. Although, you are right, she wasn't much older than Jessie when we last saw her. Ah... here it is. Look!" She passed a photograph to Jack who looked at it carefully, before grumbling and handing it back to Helen.

"Look, Jessie. This is Anna and Luna."

It was an old picture, creased and tattered around the edges, but it showed a beautiful grey horse leaping over a huge fence. He looked healthy and powerful. His rider, a young girl, was dressed smartly and in the background could be seen a crowd of people.

"Is this your horse?"

"Luna. He was a beautiful horse once. Won all the competitions: showjumping, dressage, eventing, but he's getting old now. He's not looking his best and I can't really... I don't have the time... It's just not easy to do everything." Helen looked at Jack again and took a deep breath.

"Do you still have him?" Jessie asked, hoping that the lie wouldn't show in her voice.

"Well, yes..."

"Can I help you with him perhaps?" Jessie couldn't believe her luck that her plan had worked.

"Oh, Jessie. I don't know. He's really very old now and he's not an easy horse..."

"It's okay. I've looked after horses before." Lies on top of more lies.

"Really?"

"Yeah, I looked after lots of horses before we moved down here."

"Well, okay, maybe that would be good. Only, not now it'll be dark soon and you should be getting back. Come back tomorrow morning and you can meet Luna."

Jessie couldn't stop grinning on the walk home. She felt dizzy with excitement and happier than she had been for days, ever since... She pushed all the bad stuff, the painful thoughts, out of her mind and just focussed on Luna. She remembered the old photograph, Luna as he was in that picture: bright, alert and healthy.

She imagined that it was herself in Anna's place in the picture. She could feel the summer breeze on her face, the leather reins in her hands and her heart hammering in her chest as Luna hung in mid-air over the show jump. His mane fluttering over her fingers. The crowds cheering. The smell of crushed grass and sweet hay. A moment frozen in time as the photographer pressed the button on his camera. One day, it would be her in that picture, nobody else.

Chapter 3

Jessie lay awake all night. She had left her bedroom curtains open and watched the patch of sky gradually lighten. When the first rays of sunlight appeared over the horizon, Jessie pulled on a jumper and went to sit on the window ledge. The excitement from the night before had turned into an anxious fluttering. When she had finally got back from Helen and Jack's, her mum had been furious. She had been out looking for Jessie and was just about to call the police, fearing that her daughter had fallen off a cliff or been kidnapped.

"Get up to your room this instant," she had raged as Jessie scuttled upstairs and flung herself onto the bed.

That had been the last she had seen of her mother and the thought of vanishing again, right now, of dashing across the moors to the horse who was waiting for her, was both appealing and terrifying. She had thought about it all night. As she sat on the window ledge, watching the day slowly wake up, she knew she must wait. She needed another plan, one which would allow her to go out, on her own, whenever she wanted.

Megan's cries came through the gap under the door and the sound was followed moments later by her mum's footsteps on the landing. The hall light switched on with a click and yellow light spilled through the gap under Jessie's door. Jessie pulled her knees against her chest and watched the light pool around the dark alcoves and glitter on the nails in the bare floorboards. Without knowing why, Jessie felt herself holding her breath as Megan was quickly soothed and her mum's soft footsteps returned and then stopped outside Jessie's own bedroom door.

"What are you doing up?" her mum whispered as she pushed open the door, allowing the hall light to flood Jessie's dark room. Jessie shook her head, wriggling back further into the shadows.

Her mum came in, shut the door behind her and walked over to lean against the ledge Jessie was sitting on. In the dim light, her mum's face looked older, there were dark patches under her eyes and lines across her forehead that Jessie had not noticed before.

"I'm sorry I shouted at you, love," her mum murmured, reaching out to stroke Jessie's fringe away from her eyes.

"I was just so worried and scared that something had happened. I love you so much, you know that don't you?"

Jessie nodded.

"I, I just... I made some friends and lost track of time." Jessie whispered.

"Some friends? That's nice."

Jessie could see her mum's mind working, realising that by making friends here it might make Jessie less likely to want to leave.

"Who are these friends?"

Jessie had always been a smart girl. When she was two, she realised that if she cried loudly enough and for long enough, her parents would give into her every demand. When she was seven, she learned that if her parents said no to something she wanted, she only had to wait until the next weekend when she saw her grandmother and ask her instead. By eleven, Jessie had become a master at thinking through a situation and turning it to her favour. Despite the anger that still gripped a fist inside her, Jessie wanted, more than anything, to be able to see Luna again and knew that she needed a plan in order to do so.

"Just some kids. I thought they might be in my class when I start school after the summer."

Jessie could have predicted the sigh of relief and the way her mother's tense features softened.

"So you understand that this is home for us now? No going back?"

"Yeah, I know that."

Even the fake admission twisted a knot in her stomach and Jessie pictured her Dad in bed, propped up against the pillows, reading glasses on, paperback in hand. She imagined him glance up from the book, eyes watching her over the lenses. The expression on his face slowly changing from surprise to sadness.

***

As the morning passed by, breakfasts were eaten, teeth brushed, decisions made about whether it was warm enough for shorts; Jessie began to lose all hope of being able to escape on her own to see Luna. There was no way her mum would let her go off anywhere by herself and if she suggested they go together, then all her lies to Helen would be revealed and that would be the end to her dreams of a summer spent riding and grooming and gaining Luna's trust.

She went outside and sat on the rope swing tied to an old yew tree and thought and swung. With each swing and each thought, the real world seemed to blur. Backwards and forwards. Jessie liked the way she could catch a glimpse of the shining sea with each swing upwards. With her head tilted backwards and the rush of air in her ears, it took her a few moments before she noticed the clip-clop of hooves on tarmac. With a few more swings higher Jessie caught sight of the bright fluorescent yellow tabards of two riders coming down the lane.

It seemed like fate. There was a girl and a boy who were about her age. The girl rode a stocky, black cob with a white star on its forehead and four white socks. The boy rode a bay pony. With each swing upwards, looking over the top of the hedge, Jessie caught glimpses of the riders: laughing together, teeth bright white in the sunshine. Blonde hair and blue t-shirts. A riding crop being trailed lazily through the privet hedge. Two pairs of eyes looking upwards with surprise.

"Hello!" the boy called.

It was only then that Jessie realised how ridiculous she must have looked. Her head bobbing up and down behind the hedge. She felt embarrassed but also knew that this was her one chance of getting out and visiting Luna. She leapt off the swing and ambled over to lean carelessly against the garden gate.

"Alright?" she asked, trying to act cool yet she could feel the heat that had flooded to her face.

"Hi." The girl replied.

"I like your horses."

"You can come and stroke them if you like."

"Thanks."

Jessie tried to smooth her hair which had got all tangled from the swinging and walked through the gate. It felt as though she had passed between two worlds - the loneliness of the garden onto the sunny path where the scent of warm horses and the sounds of jingling tack and squeak of leather felt so familiar to Jessie, even though this was all new to her. She could almost have believed that she had told her mum the truth - as the ponies pricked their ears and stretched their necks in Jessie's direction, it was as though she was meeting new friends.

"Hello." She murmured and the black pony breathed warm air over her fingers, raising his whiskery nose to nuzzle at her face. Jessie forgot all about pretending to be cool and grinned.

"Do you keep them near here?" Jessie asked, excitedly.

"Yeah, not far."

"Can I come back with you?"

The two children exchanged unsure looks but could not think of an excuse quickly enough and nodded.

"Hang on a sec."

Jessie dashed inside.

In the house she explained to her mum that the children she had met the day before had asked if she would like to go up to the stables with them. It wasn't far away, just down the road, and she would be perfectly safe. She wouldn't stay long, no more than a couple of hours and she would definitely be back in time to tidy her bedroom and help make the dinner.

"It's nearly lunchtime. You'll be hungry."

Jessie grabbed an apple from the fruit bowl. Her mum smiled at her and opened the front door wide to see the children for herself. She raised a hand and waved at them. They waved shyly in return.

"Alright. Fine. But be careful. And not too long."

Jessie was already out of the door and following the horses up the road. It had all worked out perfectly, Jessie thought as she listened to the swish of the black pony's thick tail as he batted away a fly and the jingle of the metal curb chain on the bridle of the bay. It seemed as though it were meant to happen. She could go with these two, show a bit of interest for ten minutes or so and then wander off, across the moors to see Luna. She would be a bit later than she had planned and she hoped that Helen wasn't getting angry at having to wait for her.

The yard was busy with people everywhere. A lady in pink jodhpurs was carefully manoeuvring a wheelbarrow full of manure up a steep muck heap. Three young children were clambering around in the hay barn. A girl was having a lesson on a chestnut Arab in a grassy paddock. Two teenage girls giggled as they walked past, they wore the same blue t-shirts which, Jessie noticed, were emblazoned with the riding school's name embroidered in gold thread.

"Legs, legs, legs, sit up straight, heels down, toes in," the instructor's booming voice drifted across on the warm air.

The girl and the boy, 'Lauren and Nathan', as Jessie had learnt on the walk over, tied their horses to a rail and took off their hats - their hair stuck up at funny angles and Jessie had to bite her lip to stop herself laughing.

It was like another world to Jessie, full of things she knew nothing of, yet was desperate to learn about. She wanted to be part of this world of ponies and sweet smelling hay: the warm sun, the birds singing and the rolling green hills that dropped away to the sea. She wanted to learn the foreign language full of words like 'numnah,' 'dandy brush' and 'chaff.'

Jessie spent the next half an hour helping Lauren with the black pony, Charlie. They sponged off the area where his saddle had been, picked out his hooves, mixed up his feed and finally watched him trot across the field whinnying to the other three horses already peacefully grazing. Jessie discovered that Charlie had been a birthday present from her parents two years ago. Lauren had woken up to a head collar wrapped in shiny blue paper, been blindfolded and driven to the yard to find Charlie standing in his stable. Jessie could not help but feel a little jealous.

"Oh, there's mum." Lauren said as a shiny black range rover bounced down the track towards the yard, "Do you want a lift home?"

"No, that's okay," Jessie said, her heart already beginning to race at the thought of her own secret horse who she was ready to visit.

***

Helen opened the door. She looked red faced and flustered, her clothes were dusty and her hands shaking slightly.

"Oh Jessie, hello!"

Helen led Jessie down the garden path and out of a gate at the back which led into the barns.

"I've been having some trouble. I know nothing about horses; see, Luna was Jack's horse, he was the one who had grown up with them. Luna, well, he went away for a while, but he's back now and I really should try to sell him but I just can't bring myself to... after everything he's been through. Poor lad."

Out on the yard, Luna's stable door was wide open and the paddock gate was swinging on its hinges.

"I wanted to tidy him up a bit before you got here but he dashed out of the stable as soon as I opened the door," Helen explained, "I've already tried to catch him but can't get near. Here, take this lead rope, you might have more luck, just be careful though."

Jessie took the rope. Luna was standing at the far end of the paddock, his nostrils flared and sides heaving. Jessie thought, if he saw the rope he would know that she was going to catch him so instead she coiled up the rope and tucked it inside her jacket. She walked out through the gate into the paddock.

Luna continued to stand watching Jessie, as she slowly approached. He was so thin; his ribs and hips jutted out and his eyes looked sunken. His mane and tail were sparse where they had been rubbed. Blood and sweat had matted his coat. Yet, despite all of this, there was still a spark in his eyes - he had obviously been a beautiful creature once.

As Jessie got close to Luna, his body tensed and with her next step forwards he set off cantering to the other corner of the field. Jessie thought again, it was useless her walking up to him; he would just run away again. She had to make him curious in her - he had to want to come to her.

She stopped watching Luna and turned her back on him. She remembered the uneaten apple in her pocket and started to dig her fingers into it to break it into pieces. She glanced over her shoulder and saw that Luna was watching her intently. She took a few steps sideways, avoiding all eye contact with him, as soon as he thought about moving away she stopped.

Gradually, in this way, Jessie was able to edge close enough to Luna to be able to hear his breathing. She slowly moved her hand offering a piece of apple and waited for him to take the next step. He was too interested to resist and closed the space between them.

Jessie still avoided eye contact with him but allowed herself a little smile as she felt his soft, whiskery muzzle take the apple from her hand. With this contact made, she moved sideways up to him and he allowed her to stroke his chest.

"Hello, old boy," she murmured, gently stroking the white hair as Luna nuzzled at her pockets for another piece of apple.

Jessie looked up into his sad, brown eyes and knew that this was just the beginning of their adventure together.

Chapter 4

The next weekend, Jessie found herself walking alongside Lauren and Charlie as they left behind the noise and chaos of the busy yard and hacked out to the moors. Jessie scampered ahead, jumped from boulder to boulder, lagged behind and ran to catch up. She watched Lauren's purple riding helmet bobbing about up ahead and the sun gleam off her shiny jodhpur boots with a knot of envy in her chest. She made herself feel better by imagining the day when she would be riding Luna up here. Instead of her tatty trainers and frayed shorts, she pictured herself wearing jodhpurs, chaps and smart boots. Luna would be fit and healthy, his white coat gleaming and the breeze fanning his tail. They would gallop across the moors, jump bushes and fences and never stop until they reached the sea.

She just needed time. Time and patience. Jessie had plenty of time, it was nearly the summer holidays, but patience had never been Jessie's strong point. She always wanted everything right away, she wasn't prepared to wait, to work hard and to hope that good things would come her way. Perhaps, however, in this quiet place where nothing much seemed to happen, she could learn to be patient and to work for the things she wanted.

Jessie ran on ahead to the brow of a hill and stood on a boulder. It was a clear day and she could see for miles all around. The moorland curved and

~ 37 ~

dipped and finally dropped away to the sea. The land covered in bracken and yellow gorse with the hard white granite rocks that jutted through the soft foliage. The path curved around the side of a steep hill and Jessie could see, on the far side, there was a lake gleaming in the sunshine.

"Hey, look!" Lauren said as they approached. Cupped at the foot of bowl shaped hills, the lake glittered like a jewel, fringed by coarse, spiky reeds and mossy boulders. Lauren pointed to a spot on the far side: sheltered by the hills, a level stretch of grass and a tumbledown stone building. Somebody had lashed together a couple of pieces of corrugated iron to form a makeshift roof and outside there were two rusting metal garden chairs. The girls' footsteps crunched on the shale as they followed the path towards the hut.

A steep hillside sheltered the building and warmed the breeze that skittered across the lake surface, creating little ripples and eddies in the clear water. Jessie tentatively sat down on one of the garden chairs, testing it cautiously at first and then more confidently settling back into the fabric when she realised that it was not going to break. The air smelt of the sea and the warmth made her feel sleepy as she looked up into the deep blue sky.

Lauren had left Charlie eating at the water's edge and was already poking her head inside the hut.

"I wonder who brought all this stuff up here?" she said, "there's an old barbecue or something, and newspapers and a kettle. Do you think someone's living here?"

"Nah," Jessie said, "who would live here?"

"I don't know," said Lauren "maybe some old tramp, or a witch... or a ghost," she grabbed hold of the back of the chair Jessie was sitting on and shook it playfully, trying to frighten her.

Jessie pushed her away and went inside the hut to look for herself. It was cold and damp with slime trails from slugs and snails glittering on the walls. There was one hole in the wall facing the lake which formed a rough window and in the middle of the earthen floor there was an upturned crate, used as a table with the barbecue and kettle on top. Jessie poked at the grey ash and smeared it across Lauren's face, Lauren leapt away with a squeal.

"It's been used. Someone must have been up here quite recently."

There were pieces of cardboard on the floor in one corner and a sleeping bag, a carrier bag of empty packaging, newspapers and candles were strewn about carelessly. A chipped mug, half used packet of sugar and several teabags lay inside a plastic washing up bowl.

"Bet you wouldn't dare to come up here at night-time. I bet you wouldn't come here on your own," teased Lauren.

"Yeah, of course I would."

"Yeah, right. Imagine being here in the dark," Lauren shuddered.

Jessie thought of the dark, hidden places back in her old home town. The homeless man with a scruffy dog on a piece of rope who sold the Big Issue on the corner by the Spar. The benches in the park where teenage boyfriends and girlfriends sat and kissed for hours. The alleyways from which cats emerged into pools of streetlights. The shadowy car parks and pub doorways.

"We should come back another time and see who it is," Lauren said, emerging into the sunshine. Jessie followed, her eyes momentarily blinded after the dim light of the hut.

"If you like," Jessie shrugged, pretending not to care but, inside, the excitement of the adventure made her stomach flutter.

They returned to Charlie and led him away from the hut, taking the path that looped around the tor and headed for home. Far down below, as she looked out to the sea, Jessie could see Helen and Jack's farm. She could see a white shape in the field and knew it must be Luna. She was a little way ahead of Lauren and stopped for a moment. She looked at Luna and he lifted his head and seemed to look back at her. Lauren noticed and pointed,

"The horse is back!"

"Which horse?" Jessie said, casually.

"It's been ages. He's got so thin."

"Who is he?" Jessie asked, pretending not to care.

"I don't know really. Just a horse that we used to see sometimes, but he went away for ages. Mum said she thought he'd been stolen, but, he's back now, so maybe not. Something must have happened to him, though. Look, you can see his ribs and scars, even from here. It was probably that scary man."

Lauren had caught up with Jessie now and pulled Charlie up beside her.

"What scary man?" Jessie asked.

"He owns the horse. He always shouts at people and, once, we saw him wandering past our house in his pyjamas and slippers. Nathan is obsessed with coming over here. He's always trying to catch a glimpse of him through the windows."

Jessie felt angry with Nathan, and with Lauren for being so immature to laugh at an old man who was ill but, she tried to remember that neither of them knew Jack and so they couldn't be expected to understand. They didn't know that he was forgetful and easily confused. She bit her lip to stop herself from making a rude comment about Nathan's behaviour.

"Do you really think it was the owner who did that to the horse?"

The thought had been in her mind ever since she first saw Luna cowering in the back of his stable, covered in blood and sweat, panic in his dark eyes.

"I guess so."

"Poor thing," Jessie murmured and kept on walking. Her mind worked at top speed, trying to figure out what kind of people Helen and Jack really were. They seemed so kind but should she really trust them? Where had Luna gone, and Anna, the girl in the photo, if Helen and Jack were as kind as they seemed, where was Anna now? Surely she'd still be around if she cared about the Chalke's as much as it had seemed to Jessie at first.

Jessie thought of Nathan peering in at the windows of the farmhouse. She imagined Jack sitting in his chair, watching Nathan through the glass but unable to speak the words to ask him to go. With the realisation that it was possible to see right into the stable yard, even from this distance away, Jessie made a mental note to be careful. Very careful. Maybe it was just because it was such a clear day, but she would have to watch her back if she wanted to keep her time with Luna a secret.

Where the footpath met the road, Jessie opened the gate for Lauren to ride through and closed it behind her.

"I'm going to head back home," she said and Lauren turned and waved, Charlie's hooves clopping along the tarmac.

Jessie walked in the direction of home just until Lauren was out of sight and then she turned back towards the Chalke's farm.

***

All of Cornwall seemed to spread around Jessie like an open hand. Palm up to the vast expanse of sky, headlands stretching out like rough fingers and the curves of rivers and hedges like veins and lines on old hands. Practical, hard working hands that had dug holes and hauled ropes and mended fences. Grey and purple clouds chased across the blue sky as Jessie walked beneath. She felt so small and insignificant, just one spark of life amongst all the other living things she was surrounded by: birds, insects, plants, humans, everything was equal out here in the wild landscape of moors and sea.

Polgwidden, Jessie's new home, grew slowly smaller. Clustered around the beach, the town gleamed white, the seagulls fluttered like bunting strung across the harbour. The yellow curve of sand. Jessie could almost taste the vanilla ice cream and hear laughter drifting up from behind the striped windbreaks. She already knew some of the town's inhabitants; of Jim who worked in the post office and was also the quizmaster at the pub quiz each Thursday. Mary and Brenda ensured that every old lady who visited their hairdressers came out with identical blue rinsed perms and a roundup of the week's village gossip. Cora ran the post office and walked her two Shih-Tzu dogs along the beach first thing each morning. Luke, the young postman, swam in the sea every evening.

Jessie left them all behind as she walked across the lonely moors with just the birds for company. The herd of ponies kept a close eye on her. Their dark, shiny eyes which seemed to know the truth. It was as though they had seen this all before and knew just how it would end.

Jessie knocked on the blue door to Helen and Jack's house. Helen was pleased to see her and ushered her out to the yard.

"Luna's much happier," she said, excitedly.

"Really?"

"Yes, my daughter and her husband came over, they fixed the fencing so he can go out in the paddock now. Of course, they had an ulterior motive."

Out in the paddock, grazing near Luna was a little chestnut Shetland. He was everything Luna was not; where Luna was thin, the pony was fat, Luna's eyes were nervous and wary, the pony's bright and interested. When the pony moved too near to Luna, Luna lifted his head, flattened his ears and with wrinkled nostrils and bared teeth, scared him back to a suitable distance. Despite this, there was something more relaxed about Luna's posture, he seemed calmer and more content than before.

On hearing Jessie and Helen approach, the pony looked up and whinnied a greeting.

"This is Bob," said Helen.

Bob trotted over to the fence, his sparky black eyes half hidden by a thick tousled forelock. His coat was shiny and he looked so full of life that Jessie couldn't help but smile.

"My daughter bought him for Amber, my granddaughter. She's lost interest now though so I've ended up with yet another being to take care of."

Luna held back warily, the whites of his eyes showed as he watched Helen and Jessie nervously. Bob tossed his head as he waited for the carrot that he was certain must be coming his way. There couldn't be a bigger difference between the two horses; one who knew no bad in humans and the other who knew too much.

"Can I groom Bob?" Jessie asked. She had watched Lauren closely as she prepared Charlie for their ride and wanted to practise for herself.

"Yes, okay, love. There's a few brushes in that barn there. Don't go near Luna though, you can help me to feed him but I don't want you getting hurt. I'll be back in the house if you need anything."

Helen turned and left Jessie alone with the two horses. She couldn't believe it, her own horses to take care of. She remembered her old house, the city she had grown up in and the streets she had walked down. They felt like a distant memory now that she was surrounded by fields and sky. The sound of sparrows twittering in the trees, the drone of bumblebees as they flew drowsily amongst the flowers, the warmth of the sun on her neck.

She fetched the brushes, clambered over the gate and wrapped her arms around Bob's furry neck. She breathed in the sweet smell of horse and closed her eyes.

I love you, she thought. Love in its purest form. Love for the sun on her skin, for the salty sea air, for the buzzard on the fence post and the rabbits nibbling the grass. The insects in their secret miniature world, the ivy on the stable wall, the glimmer of sea on the horizon. Her heart ached with love for it all.

As Jessie groomed Bob, she watched Luna out of the corner of her eye. He had begun to graze a few yards away but his ears kept flicking in her direction. As Jessie softly murmured words under her breath, Luna raised his head to look at her before returning to the grass. Bob enjoyed all the attention, his top lip twitching as Jessie scratched his withers.

Jessie laughed.

"Is that nice, eh?" she held out a hand and Bob began to nuzzle at it gently. Luna kept his distance. As adorable as Bob was, there was something in Luna's aloof, nervous nature that Jessie recognised. A connection, something that seemed familiar to her, as though she were looking in a mirror at a part of her own personality.

She edged up to Luna and stopped just within touching distance. She breathed in deeply; the scent of gorse and sea and summer all around her. She felt her feet on the earth, felt rooted to the soil like a great oak tree. She felt calm, relaxed and stretched out her hand. In that moment, Luna, too, stretched out his neck and breathed on her fingers. Jessie wanted to touch him, to put tack on him, to gallop him across the beach. She wanted to jump the highest fences and ride to the top of the rocky tors on the moorland. Yet, in that one moment of stillness, she also knew that, just this once, she must be patient.

She turned and left. Leaving Bob to return to grazing and Luna to watch her go.

Chapter 5

Jessie returned the brushes to the barn and walked along the flagstone path towards the farmhouse. Through the misty window, she saw Jack seated in his old chair. His sharp eyes, magnified behind thick spectacles, were surrounded by a web of deep wrinkles. His papery thin skin looked grey through the windowpane and his white hair was wispy and unbrushed. Behind him, the room was dim, a blue light flickered in the glass and gave Jessie the impression that the television was on. Jessie wondered what he was watching. A programme about antiques, perhaps? Some old war film?

Jack was ignoring whatever it was on the TV and, instead, he stared intently out of the window. His eyes were stern, his jaw clenched and the expression on his blank face made Jessie feel nervous and a little frightened. She knew that he was ill and he would not behave in the same way that other people did, he was unpredictable, but Lauren's suggestion earlier that day kept returning. *Had he been the one to cause the bloody gashes on Luna's neck?* She kept walking closer to the house, all the while Jack watched her every step.

"I'm off now," she called through the open door.

"Oh, Jessie," Helen shuffled up to the front door, wiping her floury hands on her apron, "thank you for coming today..."

Helen's words were suddenly cut off by a loud, piercing whinny coming from the field, then the sound of hoof beats and finally they saw Luna frantically galloping around the field. His screams were high pitched and terrified and he moved as though he were being chased by wolves or bears or any other predator that horses still imagine in their instinctive minds when something startles them. In a flash, Jack was at the door. He could move surprisingly fast for an old man and before Helen was able to stop him he was out of the door and heading down the path.

"What's he going to do?" Jessie cried.

"Don't worry," Helen said, catching hold of Jessie's arm and following Jack towards the yard.

"He's going to hurt him!"

"No. He won't."

Jack flung open the yard gate and Luna whinnied even louder when he saw Jack approach. Jack walked calmly and slowly and Luna also calmed. He dashed up to Jack's side and walked just a few paces behind him. Jack stopped. Luna stopped. Luna moved closer and dropped his nose to Jack's waist and Jack reached out a hand to rub Luna's forehead. Luna seemed to calm instantly and, to Jessie, it looked like magic.

"I wish I could do that," she breathed.

Jack kept on walking towards the stone hedge.

"What's he seen?" Helen murmured from where she stood beside Jessie. Jessie could not make out anything. Luna was staring intently at something that must be behind the hedge. A few shadows slowly drifted across the moorland behind and the wind rippled through the soft green leaves of the stunted trees. A few tall purple foxgloves and a splash of yellow lichen on the stone hedge caught Jessie's eye but she could not make out anything that would have caused such a reaction in Luna.

Jack slowly, silently, leant against the stone hedge and, with a quick grab, he reached down and caught hold of a boy who had been hiding. Jessie could not hear the words but she could tell that Jack was shouting angrily as the boy twisted and wriggled and was quickly out of Jack's grasp and running away over the hills. Jessie saw a flash of blond hair and, as he ran, she realised with a start that she recognised his blue t-shirt. It was the riding school kit - bright blue with the silver logo.

'*Nathan*.' Jessie thought, '*please don't let him have seen me.*'

Her time with Luna had only just begun; it was too early for the secret to be out already.

***

When Jessie got home her mum had made sandwiches for lunch and ushered everybody into the sunny garden. Inside the house, everything still felt strange. Half unpacked boxes spilled out their contents, reminders of their old life. There was an air of sadness, of tears that had been quietly sobbed into pillows. A sadness which seemed intensified by the dust and the dim light. Always a memory of her dad holding that mug, the dish towel, the vase, putting away that pan and cleaning the mirror.

Outside, however, everything felt fresh and new. The sadness faded amidst the birdsong and bright colours of wild flowers in their overgrown jungle-garden. The normality of her family laughing and chatting together made Jessie forget everything for a while. The summer sunshine and the memory of grooming Bob and discovering the hut and the way Luna had calmed when he saw Jack made her feel happy. All worries about Nathan and whether he had seen her quickly disappeared and she could not stop a huge grin from breaking out on her face and a loud laugh escape as Matthew told some silly joke. She felt instantly guilty as thoughts of her dad, sat on the sofa in their old flat, watching football on his own, clouded her thoughts.

"It's good to see you smile, Jess," her mum said, gently.

Her perfectly made up face was shaded by a large, floppy hat and her eyes hidden behind a pair of dark glasses. She seemed too glamorous to be sitting here, amongst the weeds, although Jessie knew that the hat hid her unwashed hair and the sunglasses her puffy eyes. As they were clearing away the plates, crusts thrown to the birds who instantly squabbled over them in a flurry of feathers and chirps, Lauren arrived at the front door. Jessie was reminded of Nathan and the way he had been so close to discovering her secret that afternoon, Jessie wondered whether he had told his sister anything but Lauren seemed relaxed and happy, a twinkle gleaming in her eyes as she hoisted the rucksack on her back into a more comfortable position.

"Hello, it's lovely to meet you properly," Jessie's mum said, opening the door.

"Hi," Lauren smiled, her big blue eyes looked the picture of innocence.

"Can Jessie come to our house for a sleepover?" she asked, excitedly. There was a mischievous look on her face and Jessie knew that it was not the house she was planning on staying at. The rucksack was a big giveaway.

"Well, I don't know."

"Please? Mum is expecting her now and has made a big cake and I'll look after her."

"Jess? Do you want to go?"

Lauren nodded and mimed a ghost behind Jessie's mum's back. She was planning on going up to the hut and Jessie knew that she could not back down now so agreed.

***

They walked along in single file in the direction of the hut, Jessie lagging behind as Lauren marched on ahead. It was still bright daylight but the sun was beginning to sink lower and the air had grown a little cooler. Jessie carried a bag on her back with her pyjamas and toothbrush and held her sleeping bag under her arm. As they walked Jessie thought of all of the things that she should have brought with her for a night outside: food, drink, a torch,... something to scare away ghosts. What did scare away ghosts? *Nothing*, Jessie thought, as they walked along, growing increasingly nervous.

"Where did you tell your mum you were going?" Jessie asked Lauren.

"To yours!" Lauren replied, turning to grin at Jessie.

The sun had dropped below the tor as they reached the hut and a low mist was beginning to creep across the water. The hills had turned a darker colour and an earthy smell of soil and bracken rose up as the girls footsteps crushed the leaves of plants growing along the path. There was no sign of anybody else; no marks on the soft mud by the lake's edge, everything just as it had been earlier that day.

The hut itself was even more bleak than before. Inside, the walls were wet to touch and the floor was squidgy to walk on. Jessie peered inside. Everything looked the same, except, she noticed, there was a paper envelope left on an upturned crate.

"Hey, look!" Jessie said, taking the envelope out into the fading daylight and looking inside. It contained photographs of the sea and moorland surrounding them: rocks, trees, clouds, each picture perfectly capturing the wild, lonely beauty of the landscape.

"Well, it's probably not a ghost then," said Lauren, "I can't imagine a ghost taking pictures."

"You didn't really think it was, did you?" Jessie asked, but Lauren only smirked and shrugged her shoulders.

"Do you still want to stay?" Jessie asked. A real person staying in this hut was actually more frightening to her than a ghost. The fantastical idea of a couple of kids pretending to be ghost-hunters camping out in a haunted hut was an adventure, but sleeping rough in a hut where another person could turn up at any moment was something else.

"Yeah... course..." Lauren said, hesitantly. "That's only if you do. Of course, if you'd rather not, then we can always go back to my house, Mum won't mind, she'll make dinner and we can watch some films and eat popcorn," Lauren waffled, hopefully.

"No," said Jessie, not wanting to be the one to chicken out, "we might as well stay, now that we're here."

The two girls ate the odd items of food that Lauren had managed to secretly grab from the kitchen when her mum's back was turned; handfuls of dry cornflakes from a half empty packet, a lump of Cheddar cheese, ginger biscuits and a big block of milk chocolate. They drank orange juice straight from the carton and by the time they had finished the sky had turned an inky purple. The big white face of the moon had crept up over the hills and sparkled on the lake's surface. The girls suddenly felt very alone, with no distant glimmer of streetlights and civilisation, just the sound of the breeze and the lapping water.

"Jessie?" Lauren said quietly, breaking the silence which had fallen over them.

"Yeah?"

"Do you like it in Cornwall? Or do you think you will go back to your old house?"

Jessie felt so confused, her mind was muddled, she knew that she wanted to spend more time with Luna. She liked the freedom she felt when she was out on the moors, she liked the sound of the sea and the way she could sit on the window ledge in her bedroom and watch the ponies and the birds flying all around her. And yet, to stay would mean to leave behind all those memories of her old life, all the Christmases and the weekends, the memories of her old school and her friends. Even if her dad were to decide to move to Cornwall, there would still be so much that would gradually fade and be lost to her.

"I don't know," she replied, honestly, "sometimes I want to stay and sometimes I want to go back."

"Well, I hope you stay," said Lauren and Jessie could just about make out the gleam of her teeth in the darkness.

The two girls spread the cardboard out on the floor of the hut and unrolled their sleeping bags. They wriggled down into the warmth and lay quietly listening to the hushed sounds of nature just outside: water, wind, trees, leaves. It seemed like the Earth was breathing and the idea was comforting to Jessie. She forgot about her mum at home, watching a film on TV, glancing at her phone every few minutes to check that Jessie hadn't tried to call her. She forgot about Luna, resting a hoof as he half-dozed beside Bob who lay on his side, fast asleep. She forgot about her dad, at the pub, flirting with a barmaid. She forgot about Matthew and Megan; both fast asleep under clean, new bed linen. With a still, clear mind, Jessie drifted off into a peaceful sleep.

***

"What was that?" Jessie was awoken with a start by Lauren, prodding her through her sleeping bag, "Jessie, wake up. I heard a noise."

Lauren was on her feet, crouching near the doorway. A black shape pressed against the wall and framed by a bright sunrise. She kept a hand to her stomach as if holding a breath inside herself, and tried to peer around the edge to see what was outside. Jessie was too tired and her sleeping bag too cosy. She had been having the best dream, about swimming in the sea on Luna's back, and she wanted to return to it.

"It was nothing, it's too early," she said, turning over and about to pull the sleeping bag over her ears. However, before she could, she heard it.

The click of a camera.

"There it is again!" said Lauren.

The clicking sounds continued and then the heavy slip-slide of footsteps across the pebbly shale near the lake. Jessie crawled out of her sleeping bag, her heart racing. She smoothed her hair away from her face and, silently, reached for her shoes.

"We should go and have a look," she said, but Lauren shook her head, frantically.

"No, I don't think we should," she whispered, "it might still be a ghost."

"It's not a ghost."

"Well, even if it is a person, they might be angry that we've been spying on them."

"They'll probably come in here anyway to collect their photos."

"Oh no," Lauren squealed in terror, "I had forgotten about that."

The moments that followed could only have been minutes, but they felt like hours to Jessie and Lauren who crouched in the shadows of the hut. Their legs grew stiff and their toes tingled with pins and needles, but neither girl could bring themselves to move any closer to the doorway for fear of being spotted. Gradually, the sound of footsteps became quieter and Jessie let go of the breath she had been holding as it became clear that the person was not intending on returning to the hut.

"Let's go and have a look," said Jessie.

Outside there was no sign of anybody. The lake was still and calm, the sky dotted with a few grey clouds. On the far side of the lake, the seven wild ponies dozed by the water's edge. The girls dashed down to the shore, unkempt hair blowing about their faces and clothes creased, the peered over the marks in the sand and could see footprints.

"There was someone!" said Jessie, crouching down, fingers pressing into the sand on either side of the footprint, examining it like a detective, trying to learn more about their mystery owner.

"Well it definitely wasn't a ghost, then," Lauren grinned.

"Nope, not unless the ghost wears trainers," said Jessie, pointing out a logo that could just be seen pressed into the wet sand. They looked all around them for some other sign, but there was nothing. The ponies looked only at Jessie and Lauren with no glance to another stranger that could be up in the hills by now. The birds swooped and called in the same way that they always did at this time in the morning; their day beginning with a constant search for food for their chicks, cosy in their nests. There was no litter, no forgotten jacket, no sign at all apart from the line of footprints which were quickly lost as the sand turned to earth.

Chapter 6

The days passed and the following Saturday after dinner, as soon as her mum had gone upstairs to put Megan to bed, Jessie was quietly pulling on her socks and shoes once more. Matthew looked at her from the living room.

"Where are you going now?"

"Shhh," Jessie whispered, "I won't be long. Don't tell Mum."

The plan had been hatched the previous weekend, as they packed away their sleeping bags and the remains of the food packets, Lauren had decided that they should leave a note and come back the following weekend to see if there was a reply.

Jessie opened the door and felt the cool evening air on her face. From the bathroom above, she could hear her mum chatting away in cooing baby talk to Megan. She could see the perfumed steam billowing out of the window and hear the splashing of water as Megan wriggled in the bath tub. She could imagine Megan's squirming body amongst the bubbles, the light from the bare lightbulb gleaming off the sink, sparkling in the mirror. Jessie pulled her jumper tightly around her, freeing her hair from the collar. She kept watch down the lane and as soon as she heard the clip clop of metal shoes on tarmac, she dashed out into the street to follow Lauren and Charlie.

As they passed by gardens, they heard birds twittering amongst the trees and bushes, in a final dash for the peanuts in the wire feeders before it was time for bed. Inside houses, lights were being switched on and curtains drawn. Through an open window, Jessie could hear the metallic clatter of cutlery as a table was laid for dinner. A few streetlamps were casting an orange glow on the cars parked underneath them and a ginger cat sat in a doorway surveying his kingdom before setting out for the evening patrol.

They were soon past the houses and making their way through the gate and out onto the coastal footpath. The gate creaked on its hinges as Jessie closed it behind them. They had escaped! Out from the watchful eye of the village, they headed across the moors, veering away from the sea and out towards the rocky tor, which was their landmark to show them the way to the hut.

"Do you think there will be a reply?" Lauren asked excitedly.

"Shouldn't think so," replied Jessie. Inside a mixture of nerves and excitement were swirling in her stomach.

"I wonder who it is. Maybe they're famous. They've come down to Cornwall because they don't want everybody to know who they are. Or maybe it's some romantic artist who is taking pictures of home for the person they love, who is away... far away... with no internet or phone signal."

Jessie smiled at Lauren's fantastical imagination. They had tried to think up a good note to write to the mysterious person, but in the end, Lauren had said, there was really only one thing they needed to know. *'Are you a ghost?'* scrawled in her spidery handwriting on the corner of the scrap of paper.

What sort of ghost would answer 'yes' anyway, thought Jessie, as she dashed ahead to catch the first sight of the hut from around the corner. The lake glittered and gulls swooped like scraps of paper blown about on the breeze.

"See anything?" Lauren called.

"Not yet," Jessie replied, balancing on a lump of granite and shielding her eyes from the low sun's rays.

The girls made their way down the path in silence. When they got to the bottom, Lauren leapt from Charlie's back and, tying a knot in his reins, left him to eat at a patch of grass. She scampered up to Jessie and clung onto her sweatshirt as both girls took the last few steps up to the hut's entrance.

Huddling together, they nervously peered around the door frame and breathed a sigh of relief. There was nobody there. However, when they went inside a little further they saw that a photo had been left on the wooden crate that acted as a table. Lauren picked it up and turned to Jessie.

"What is it?"

Lauren looked puzzled and handed it to Jessie. The picture was of the moorland wreathed in white mist. The mist pooled around granite rocks and gorse bushes, giving everything a ghostly appearance. However, standing tall and strong, the mist lapping at his feet, stood a stout pony. He stared directly at the camera, his eyes glistening and his mane blowing in the same direction as the tree that he stood in front of. The camera could pick out the hairs of his coat, which were slick with rain and the stems of grass that still poked out of his mouth, forgotten for a moment as his attention was caught by the camera. In a landscape that looked like a scene from a hundred years ago, where pirates could have sailed on the seas behind, where ladies could have galloped past sitting side-saddle and men peered through the open windows of their carriages, this pony would have looked just the same. Never changing. A ghost-horse, and yet solid, real, hard and muscular. His physical appearance as much a part of the landscape as the trees and the rocks and the sea.

"What does it mean?" asked Lauren, poking about amongst the cups and newspapers, but Jessie just shrugged.

"No idea," she said, but her mind was ticking through possible explanations; perhaps it meant that the stranger felt real in a world of shadows, or they were lost, in the wrong time or place; perhaps they were trying to forget about the reality of the world, trying to hide from life; or perhaps it was just a pretty picture, the photographer was having a laugh at two silly girls who had been caught up in the spirit of adventure.

"They left us some more biscuits," Lauren said picking up a packet of custard creams.

"Well, it seems ghosts shop at the Co-Op," Jessie grinned.

***

They ate a few biscuits, wrote another note *'Who are you?'* and left. Riding back along the track towards the stables, the excitement of the adventure starting to fade, a guilty ache inside her reminded Jessie that her mum would have put Megan to bed by now, she would have finished mopping up the soapy water on the bathroom floor, tidied away some of the toys left carelessly on the landing, and she would have gone downstairs, to find Jessie missing. Jessie imagined her mum looking intently into Matthew's face as he shrugged his shoulders, pacing about the kitchen, looking for a note or a sign as to Jessie's whereabouts. Despite everything, Jessie felt the twist of guilt in her stomach and the overwhelming need to get back to the cottage, to put her mum's mind at rest.

"Won't your mum be wondering where you are?" Jessie asked Lauren, hoping that she might also share the guilty feeling with her friend.

"Oh no. I told her and Nathan all about the hut and the photos and the ghost-person."

"What?! I thought that we were keeping it a secret."

"Sorry, Jess. I thought you would have told *your* mum."

A surge of wild anger rose up inside Jessie making her head feel hot and dizzy. It was not just that she felt Lauren had given away a secret that had been only theirs, but also the sudden realisation that Lauren had been the one to do the right thing. She had made the right choice, Jessie herself had made the wrong one.

"I've got to go."

Jessie started to run and kept on running, as fast as she could, until she was outside her front door. She paused for a moment. A light was on upstairs. From outside it was all calm, but Jessie knew that would change the moment she went indoors.

***

The sequence of events had unfolded just as Jessie had expected. The front door half open, Jessie kicking off her shoes, one still on as her mum appeared from the kitchen. Raised voices, cruel words and Jessie's bedroom door slammed shut. She had sat on her bed and thought about how Lauren and Nathan were probably having a good laugh about it together. She thought of Lauren the morning after the night in the hut; arriving home, tired and dusty, spilling the beans to her mum and brother and her mum chiding her softly and running her a bath; giving her clean clothes and sitting both children down in the kitchen with toast and orange juice. The summer sunshine and scent of sweet-peas streaming through the open kitchen window.

She thought of Lauren now, sitting on the sofa in the living room, her mum on one side, her brother on the other, looking at the photo of the pony on the moors, which Lauren had kept tucked inside her jacket as they rode back from the hut. She thought of the way her mum's head tilted back, her fashionable blonde haircut swinging about her face as a peal of laughter filled the room. Jessie imagined the delicious smell of dinner cooking and the way Lauren's mum gave her children's knees a squeeze before ushering them both into the kitchen.

"The perfect family," Jessie muttered darkly, as she sat in her dim bedroom, arms wrapped around bruised shins, dark hair trailing across her knees. She stared out of the window and could see a stretch of moorland beneath the darkening sky, a broad curve of purple heather, and Jessie knew that the ponies were out there somewhere. The bracken tickling their bellies and the scratch of gorse against their legs, nothing ever changing for them. Jessie pressed her face against her knees and wished, more than anything, that she were one of them.

Chapter 7

"What's Jack doing?"

Jessie sat on the sofa, stroking one of the cats that had curled up on her lap. Outside, she could see Jack slowly, carefully, shuffling past the window. He inched his way to one end of the yard, turned around and began the slow journey back again.

"He's sweeping," Helen called from the kitchen.

"Why?"

Outside, Jack straightened up and stretched the stiffness out of his back. He supported his tired muscles with outstretched hands and leaned backwards, tilting his head towards the sky and the sun. In the background, Jessie could see Luna standing at the gate watching him.

"I'm not sure really," Helen said, coming in to sit beside Jessie. "Something's changed in him since the other day when Luna came over to him. It's like he's remembered something of his old self again."

"He looks happy," Jessie said as a grin wrinkled the dry folds of skin at Jack's eyes, the sunlight glittering within.

Helen smiled and pulled her grey cardigan tightly around her, a hand resting against her chest, feeling her steady heartbeat quicken a little. "He does. Thank goodness Luna came back when he did." She sipped her tea and smiled at Jessie's surprised expression, "Yes," she said, "he arrived home not long before you."

Jessie must have looked puzzled, both at the suggestion that she had arrived home but also at the idea that Luna had not been at the farm for long.

"So that's why he was in such a terrible state," she said with a relieved sigh.

"Yes," Helen paused, "I would hate for you to think that we could cause harm to Luna in any way, and when you were worried about Jack before..."

"Oh, I know he wouldn't," Jessie felt her face getting warmer. Forgetting that she was in someone else's house for a moment, she rested her feet on the sofa cushions, wrapped her arms around her knees. "Well, for a moment perhaps I was worried."

"It's understandable," continued Helen, "I felt so ashamed for you to see Luna in such a mess, but he had only just come back a couple of weeks before."

"Where had he been?"

Helen paused for a moment but did not want to answer the question.

"Come on," she said, getting to her feet slowly and reaching out a hand to pull Jessie from the squishy cushions. "It's a story for later, not for now."

They walked outside and greeted Jack who had finished the last patch of concrete. He looked very pleased with his handiwork and patted Jessie's shoulder with a smile, pointing at the smooth yard, which was now free of muck and hay. The rusting heap of chains and tools had been stacked neatly in the barn and the drains had been cleared of the thick black gunk that had blocked them before.

"It looks much better, Jack," Jessie smiled and Jack beamed.

"Jack," Helen said, "look after Jessie for a moment, I'm going to make us a picnic. It's such a lovely day, we can sit outside and eat our sandwiches."

When Helen had gone indoors, Jack gestured to Jessie to go across the yard to the field gate. He pointed to Luna who lifted his head with a start when he saw Jessie and Jack approach. Jack fumbled with the latch on the gate and let them both into the field. He seemed urgent, desperate to show Jessie something, to teach her something that was on his mind and he knew could vanish again at any moment.

"Come on," he whispered, "over here."

"I don't know, Jack," Jessie replied, "Helen doesn't think we should go too close to Luna."

"Come on, come on. He's alright. He's a good lad really. He doesn't mean to do bad things. He just reacts, like we all do, only he's a big chap and he gets scared sometimes. But he doesn't mean it."

It was more words than Jessie had ever heard Jack speak and she felt as though he were talking about Luna and, yet, not talking about him; talking about someone else as well. Luna took a few steps closer to Jack and dropped his head, breathing heavily through flared nostrils. Luna stopped, stood upright, head held high. Jack shifted his posture, became tall, looked Luna in the eye and shooed him back.

"What are you doing, Jack?" Jessie asked, "I thought you wanted him to come to you."

Luna leapt away in a couple of bucking leaps and Jack kept moving towards him keeping his posture tall, his shoulders square. Luna trotted further away and stopped, dropped his head, turned his body away. Jack copied his behaviour and angled his body differently. It was like a dance, one that both partners understood. Each little change in body language was a word spoken between Jack and Luna.

"Come here," Jack gestured to Jessie and she moved to stand beside him, "he needs to trust you. But, also, he needs to respect you. Respect, it can't be beaten into a horse. Pain, nerves, a horse won't learn a thing if that's all he knows. But, respect can be gained by teaching him that you are a good leader. That you can be trusted to keep him safe."

Luna still stood a little distance away, his head low, body angled away from them.

"Now. Watch."

Jack guided Jessie around and they started to walk slowly away from Luna. Immediately, they heard the soft hoof-falls as Luna followed. They paused and Luna paused. They walked on and Luna started to follow again.

"Wait," said Jack.

They stopped and Luna stood just behind them. Jessie could hear his breath, could smell the sweet scent of horse, but she did not dare turn to look at him just yet.

"Turn slowly," Jack motioned and Jessie did as he said. Luna's eyes were soft and trusting and Jessie reached up and let him sniff at her hand. He let her stroke his face gently. She was quiet, afraid to say a word for fear that whatever magic was binding them together would evaporate into the warm air. When she turned again to look at Jack, her heart bursting with joy at the simple connection between horse and human, she noticed that Jack had walked back to the fence. Jessie moved to follow him and Luna came too, keeping always a couple of paces behind.

Jack's eyes were gleaming with pride and a crooked smile spread across his face when Jessie reached him.

"Thank you!" Jessie whispered.

"Well, you had to learn about horses sometime, Anna," Jack said in a voice that sounded quite unlike his old, barely used, hoarse whisper.

Jessie paused, she looked up at Jack and started to shake her head. She cleared her throat, tried to find a way to explain that she was not Anna, but it was difficult, she did not want to upset him.

"Jack, look, sorry but I'm not..." But before Jessie could speak the words, Helen appeared with a tray of sandwiches. They all squeezed onto the bench on the yard to eat their lunch, watching Luna and Bob grazing in the paddock. Jessie smiled as she remembered hearing Luna's steps following her, there had been no ropes, no head-collars: he had been with her because he wanted to be.

Jessie shuffled her feet in the dirt and traced the lines and patterns of the wooden bench with her fingertips.

"What happened to Luna before?" Jessie felt as though she needed to know. Luna had arrived back at the Chalke's farm at the same moment that Jessie, herself, had arrived in Cornwall. It seemed important.

There was quiet for some time, Jack looked sad for a moment but was quickly distracted by the gulls, soaring high in the sky with the colour of the clouds on their wings, colour of sunlight on their bellies. Helen gazed towards the paddock before taking a little breath and smiling at Jessie.

"He came back to us. After fifteen years away, can you imagine..."

Helen described in detail the events of that special morning when Luna came home, the way the window was open and the striped curtains were fluttering in the breeze, the birds seemed to be singing more loudly that usual. The radio came on and played a song that neither Helen nor Jack had heard for many years, not since they were first married and the song played in the pub at Penzance where their wedding reception was held. Helen talked about how she heard the postman's van pull up in the driveway and then drive away again. And then another vehicle, a louder engine, stopping and then driving away with the scattering sound of gravel.

"So, Luna came back," Helen finished, "Just like that. When we drew back the curtains, there he was, standing amongst the flowers. He was in such a terrible state, all the life had been drained from him and he stood there without being tied. We caught him easily and put him in the stable where he could rest and eat but, as his physical strength grew, his behaviour became worse. I didn't want to keep him in that box all the time but he was so dangerous, I couldn't get near him and, I don't really know horses, not like Jack does. He frightened me. So I just threw the feed over the door from time to time and then you came along," Helen smiled. "Our little guardian angel, appearing at just the right moment."

Jessie grinned. Perhaps it was fate. Perhaps everything that had happened was because she was *meant* to be here, to help Luna get better and to learn to trust people again.

"Can I try grooming him?" Jessie asked. Helen took her plate from her hands, stacking it with her own and Jack's, tipping the crumbs on the floor for the birds or mice.

"Only," she said, firmly, "if you are very careful. Keep to the front end and if he doesn't want to be fussed over then leave him be."

"I will," Jessie said, already dashing over to the space where the brushes were kept. She walked slowly up to Luna who lifted his head, breathed loudly but allowed Jessie to come near. She reached up to stroke his thin neck and shoulder, she noticed the way his muscles tensed as she touched him, to see him flinch at such a light touch broke Jessie's heart. She could not bear to think of what had happened to him to cause such a reaction. She continued to stroke him softly and gradually Luna relaxed, even dropping his head to nuzzle at her hair. Jessie laughed gently and scratched the patch of coat between neck and shoulder. Luna's muzzle twitched with enjoyment, his neck arching a little and shoulder dropping towards Jessie, allowing her to continue to scratch the itchy spot.

Slowly, Jessie picked up one of the brushes and, carefully, avoiding any of the sores or open wounds that still scarred his body, she gently brushed his coat. Scurf and dirt came to the surface of the white hairs and, with each rhythmic stroke, Jessie brushed it free. Luna stood with his head low, allowing her to continue to groom until the coat on his neck, shoulders and back gleamed in the sunshine. Jessie wanted to continue until all of his coat was clean, but she noticed that when she touched his belly, he stamped a hoof and the expression on his face changed, ears moving back, nostrils wrinkling, eyes widening, so she stopped.

"Good boy, good boy," she murmured as Luna moved back to Bob who was grazing near the fence. His patches of clean, white coat amongst the dirt and dried blood felt like a step in the right direction.

Chapter 8

At first, Jessie could barely look at her mum. She stared at her plate at mealtimes and the television in the evenings. She avoided catching her eye in the bathroom mirror and when her mum called to her, Jessie turned her head to indicate she had heard but kept her gaze fixed to a point in the distance. After a couple of days, she would speak to her but never more than brief answers to her questions. "Are you going to the stables?" "Yeah." "Are you ready for tea?" "Not yet." "Do you want to talk to Dad on the phone?" "No."

However, as the days went by, days spent at the farm with Luna, Jessie started to feel a little guilty. After nearly a week, Jessie made her way out into the garden where her mum was hanging the washing out to dry. Jessie picked up a peg and held it up to her.

"Sorry."

"What are you sorry for, Jess?"

"For being angry. For running off like that the other day."

"I just wish you'd be honest with me. The reason we're here is so we all have freedom. If you want to see your friends, you can. Just ask me first."

Jessie thought for a moment. She thought of Lauren and Nathan and their mum, baking cakes and giggling about ghosts and haunted huts.

"Do you want to know where we've been going?"

Her mum raised her eyebrows and nodded.

**

Later that day, with carrier bags packed with sandwiches and juice, Jessie led the way along the coast path once more. This time, her family followed. Megan bouncing about in the buggy, Matthew kicking at stones. As the land rose higher above Helen and Jack's field, her mum shouted out.

"Look at that beautiful horse, Jess!"

Jessie looked down. Luna was standing, head held high, breeze fanning his mane and tail, as he looked out to sea. For the first time since she had seen the terrified, skinny animal over the stable door, Jessie caught a glimpse of Luna as he would have been before. His neck was proud and arched, the patches of his coat that she had managed to brush free of blood and grime gleamed white in the sun. Jessie imagined herself sitting on his back. She could almost feel his mane brushing against her fingers and hear the creaking of the leather saddle.

Jessie nodded and smiled at her mum. Would she ever be able to tell her about Luna? She imagined what would happen if she were to tell her now.

'Mum, I've been looking after that horse, I've been helping his owners.' ' What? When did this happen?' 'As soon as we moved here.' ' Who are his owners?' 'A lady and a man,

Helen and Jack'. ' Do they have children?' ' No.' ' But you've been spending hours all the way out here on your own?' ' Yes.' 'Don't you know how dangerous that is?' 'It's fine, Mum.' 'It's not fine, didn't these people think to ask my permission first?' 'They think that you know' ' So you lied about that too?'

No. There was no way she could tell her mum. No way she could ever tell her. It would have to be a secret forever.

As they reached the top of the hill, Jessie looked down and saw the hut. She shielded her eyes from the sun and, if she squinted, she could just about make out a figure down by the lake. *That must be them!* she thought. The ghost-person. From this high up, Jessie couldn't make out any of their features. It was just a person, their long shadow stretching out across the sandy ground. They were standing beside the lake, looking out across the water. They seemed to sense that someone was watching and turned in Jessie's direction. Jessie, standing outlined against the sun amongst the craggy rocks and bracken, looked down, and then, in a whirling flash, the figure was gone; making their way at a fast walk around the far side of the lake and disappearing amongst the gorse bushes.

Jessie dashed down the path, leaving her family's shouts of 'Wait!' and 'Hang on a minute, Jess!" behind. She scrambled down the gravelly slope and reached the hut. Inside, a new photo, hidden inside an envelope, had been left on the table. Jessie grabbed it but didn't have time to look at it before her mum was poking her head around the doorframe.

"So this is where you've been coming," she said as Jessie hurriedly pushed the envelope into her pocket.

Jessie grinned and handed the remains of the biscuits to her brother. They spent the next hour sitting by the lake eating their sandwiches whilst Matthew skimmed stones. Jessie could feel the envelope in her pocket, it's curled edges pressing into her skin.

"Thank you for showing us this place, Jess," her mum said, turning with a look on her face, which Jessie knew meant she wanted to talk.

"It's alright," she shrugged.

"It's just... I know that things are difficult. Everything's upside down and confusing. You were close to your dad, I know that, and you're bound to miss him but he'll come down to see you soon, and you can talk to him any time you like on the phone.

Jessie had not spoken to her dad since they left. She had not felt ready to hear his familiar voice down the line. She could not bear to hear the breaks, the cracks of emotion, which she still remembered all too well from that last time she had heard it. Those final shouts, cries, sobs and then the door, slamming shut.

"In time," her mum continued, "you'll be able to go up there and he can come down here, and it will all seem so normal. As though that was the way things always were."

Her mum reached out a hand and Jessie took hold of it. She remembered how it had felt to be out on the moors on her own, to be walking up and down that path to the Chalke's farm, and the excitement and fear that she had felt the night in the hut. The feeling of being alone, very small and insignificant in this wild place. She had not realised it, but she had missed this sense of security, of not having to take care of everything by herself.

***

"Ready for your surprise?" Lauren grinned when she saw Jessie arrive at the yard. She went back into the stable block and came out leading both Charlie and a little piebald pony. She had been tacked up ready and Lauren handed Jessie both a riding helmet and the pony's reins.

"To say sorry. For spoiling our adventure last week. Her name is Fern. We can go riding together."

Jessie couldn't tell whether the odd lurching feeling in her stomach was from excitement or nerves.

"But, I can't ride. I don't know how."

"Well, you can learn. Fern's owner is away and said that we can ride her whilst she's gone."

"But will she mind me..."

"No, course not. Come on."

Lauren put her hands under Jessie's knee and on the count of three Jessie leaped and with a lot of struggling and pushing was finally sitting in the saddle. Fern stood still despite both girls laughing loudly.

"Sit up straight, heels down, toes in," Lauren instructed as they made their way down the lane and out into the open field.

"Alright, alright," Jessie muttered trying to focus on stopping Fern from heading for the nearest patch of tasty grass.

They passed through fields full of sheep that scattered as soon as they rode near and onto the coast path where the turquoise sea spread out all around them. As Jessie realised that Fern was not likely to bolt anywhere, her nerves began to fade and she started to enjoy the feeling of freedom.

Far down below, they could hear shrieks of laughter from children playing on the beach. The people looked like little colourful pebbles on the white sand as they clustered around windbreaks and stretched out on beach towels. Some swimmers in black wetsuits looked like fish splashing amongst the surf.

Jessie remembered that morning, being at the hut with her mum, Matthew and Megan. They had eaten biscuits, watched ants marching over the sandy soil, spotted black cormorants flying low and watched the clouds as they stretched and formed great animal shapes. She thought of her mum sitting on one of the rusty chairs, shielding her eyes from the sun and laughing. Her white teeth gleamed and her freckled skin seemed to glow. She didn't remember ever seeing her look so happy before - but her dad must still be so sad. Jessie's thoughts were instantly filled with images of him sitting by the open window of their flat, hot city air drifting through the gap.

The ponies plodded on. Fern followed Charlie nose to tail as they made their way along a narrow path through the heather and gorse bushes.

"We're heading for that stack of rocks over there," Lauren pointed to a granite tor in the distance. The heat from the sun made the moorland look shimmery.

"Want to try a trot?" Lauren asked, already shortening her reins.

"Okay," Jessie clenched her reins tightly, holding onto the front of the saddle. Charlie ambled into a steady trot and Jessie didn't have to do anything as Fern was certain she did not want to be left behind.

The trot was so bouncy, Jessie clutched at the saddle harder and she was jolted about with each stride.

"Try to stand up and sit down with the movement. Like this," Lauren made it look so easy but it took several attempts before Jessie got the hang of rising trot.

"Let's canter!" Lauren clicked her tongue and urged Charlie on. Jessie felt a strange mix of elation and terror as she clung to the front of the saddle, trying to get used to the rocking motion of canter. She had read lots of books about horse riding and they all said that it would take weeks of lessons before learning to canter. Yet, as the two girls raced across the moorland, nothing had felt more natural to Jessie. The seven moorland ponies watched on with black eyes from beneath their shaggy forelocks. They seemed confused at this strange behaviour from their domesticated cousins as the ponies cantered by.

When they reached the top of the hill, Jessie and Lauren came to a halt. They could see for miles all around them. From the sea, spotted with sailing boats and gannets that dropped into the blue depths, to the moors, to the rolling green fields beyond, a flock of seagulls following a tractor that bounced through the rutted soil. Jessie reached into her pocket and curled her fingers around the envelope that was tucked inside.

For a moment, she wanted to stay quiet. She wanted to keep the secret to herself so that it would be hers alone. Yet, she also felt happy from cantering across the moors with Lauren beside her. When they had first met, Lauren had simply been a good excuse to go and visit Luna. Jessie had not been interested in making friends. However, as they sat on their ponies with only the landscape surrounding them, Jessie began to think differently. Perhaps it would be nice to have some friends - that were human and her own age.

"Here," she said, reaching across the space between them and pushing the crumpled envelope into Lauren's outstretched fingers.

"Have you been back?" Lauren asked and Jessie nodded.

"I thought I should be nicer to my mum!" she grinned, "So, I showed her where we've been going."

Lauren smiled and opened the envelope. She turned it to show Jessie. The photo was of a long shadow across the pebbly shore of the lake. It must have been taken in late afternoon as the shape of the person to whom the shadow belonged was stretched out of proportion; a small round head, long body and legs. A black figure on the white pebbles. It did not give much away: there was no way to discover anything about the person from the picture.

"Did you leave another note?" Lauren asked.

"No, I didn't have time. I didn't want Mum to see."

"Well, we must go back!"

Chapter 9

The summer seemed everlasting. All thoughts of school were still weeks away and Jessie's days started to fall into a routine of going to the stables with Lauren in the morning and visiting Luna afterwards before heading home for lunch. Luna trusted her more and more as each day passed. He hardly ever bared his teeth or flattened his ears. His eyes were wide, black pools and no longer had the haunted look of fear in them. With each little improvement, Jessie wished that she could tell her mum or Lauren. She wanted to share the excitement with somebody else, however she knew that if anybody were to find out, her whole secret life with Helen, Jack and Luna would fall apart.

Over the following weeks, Jessie spent as much time as she could either at the riding stables or with Luna and Bob. At the stables, she learnt as much as she could; asking questions constantly about tack and feeding and stable management. She put all this new found knowledge to use; making sure that the paddock Luna and Bob lived in was regularly poo-picked, sorting through the hay to find the least dusty bales. She learnt the correct way to pick out hooves, put on head collars and clean bridles.

Jessie and Lauren visited the hut regularly. They left notes with question after question, but never a word was left in reply. Instead, a photograph was always left in the same place on the upturned crate.

The photo never told the girls anything about the mysterious stranger but they were always very beautiful and they were usually of local areas; a stretch of coastline, a patch of moorland, a familiar rock. With each picture the girls came up with ever more imaginative tales about who this person could be, however, there were no more signs of them. That one brief moment, when Jessie had spotted a figure down by the lake, was the one and only encounter either she or Lauren had experienced with the nameless person. A footprint, a few biscuit crumbs and the photos were the only signs that anybody else, besides themselves, had ever spent time in the little hut.

In exchange for her help around the riding stables, the instructor had given Jessie a couple of lessons for free. However, as the instructor's voice boomed at her to shorten her reins and put her shoulders back, Jessie could not help but glance across to the open moors, look out for those wild ponies she knew were watching, and wish that she were out there. The feeling of freedom, the sea breeze cooling her skin and the sense that she were as much a part of nature as the birds and the ponies and the rolling waves, it was far more thrilling to Jessie than the frustration of going round and round the school. Yet, she wanted to be a good rider. She wanted to be the best rider. That picture of the girl on Luna, jumping the coloured fence at a show remained in Jessie's head at all times.

The thoughts of shows and rosettes were still in Jessie's mind as she sidled up to Luna one Saturday morning. She would be an old lady before she even sat on his back if things continued at the snail's pace that they had all summer. With a new feeling of confidence after all the hours spent at the riding stables or out riding across the moors with Lauren; Jessie walked confidently across the field, riding helmet on, head collar in hand. Today was going to be the day.

She reached Luna and whilst he was busy nuzzling at her pockets for treats, Jessie slipped the head-collar over his nose, her fingers shaking slightly as she fastened the buckle. Luna did not seem worried at all. He stood beside her as Jessie stroked his neck and face, a warm glow spread through Jessie's body. She could do this. She began to walk and Luna followed her like a dog on a lead. If Jessie could just lead him over to the mounting block on the yard, if she could just climb onto the block, if she could just grip hold of his mane.

Luna behaved perfectly. Despite Bob's whinny of alarm at seeing his friend heading towards the stables, Luna followed Jessie calmly. It had paid off. The slow and steady pace with which she had allowed Luna time to understand that she would never do anything to harm him. It had worked. Luna walked beside her in the same way that he had followed Jack so calmly before.

Jessie remembered Jack, his chair, the window and the clear gap through which he could see the stable yard. It would be okay, Jessie thought. Jack would be glad to see Luna so relaxed. He would be proud of Jessie's horsemanship skills. She led Luna up to the mounting block and, with the memory of performing this movement so many times in the past, Luna positioned himself alongside. Jessie stood on the block, held the end of the leadrope in one hand and stroked Luna's back with the other. She felt nervous all of a sudden. Everything looked slightly different from this higher position. She could see over Luna's back to the hard, dry ground on the other side. She noticed the sharp little stones that would be painful if she fell. Luna's back looked slippery, his muscles twitching and tensing under her fingers, so different to the comfortable, solid feeling of hopping up into the deep saddle on Charlie's broad back. Jessie leant across Luna's back for a moment to test his reaction to taking her weight. He stood quietly but his head was held high and alert, ready to move at a moment's notice. Finally, with one deep breath and a quick leap, Jessie took the plunge and scrambled onto Luna's back.

Luna tensed for a moment but stood still. Without a saddle to get in the way, Jessie could feel his heart beating against his ribs. She could feel each breath he took. The softness of his mane against her fingers. The cotton rope in her hands. She felt unsteady, elated and a long, long way from the ground. The sparrows twittered in the guttering and one of

Helen's cats stretched and rolled in the sun. The stripe of sea glittered on the horizon. From being just this little higher up, Jessie could see over the stone hedges into neighbouring fields, a back garden with a paddling pool, down the lane to the village.

For one perfect moment, the world seemed to stop. Jessie did not hear the sound of cars, there was not a single person to be seen in any direction. The clouds seemed to have stopped moving overhead and the leaves on the trees paused for a second before they began, once more, to flutter on their stems. However, as quickly as time had stopped, it rushed forward again and everything seemed to happen at once. Jessie noticed two figures, high up on the moors. They were making their way down towards the farm, scampering along the rocky paths that wound around patches of bracken and gorse bushes. Jessie shielded her eyes from the sun and, as they drew near her blood turned cold as she realised that it was her brother and Nathan. What were they doing? They seemed to be coming her way. Scampering like puppies they bowled into each other, legs and arms whirling, and, as they drew near, Jessie could hear snatches of laughter and voices on the still air.

Luna's ears pricked up. His body tensed. The boys had reached the edge of the field and were clambering up, struggling to climb over the stone walls. In her panic at the sight of her brother, Jessie did not notice the signs that Luna was giving to her. She failed to see that the muscles on Luna's neck were quivering, his ears flicking frantically this way and that, his eyes wild and rolling and a thin sheen of sweat was curling the ends of his coat. He lurched forward and stopped, lurched and stopped again. Jessie slipped to one side and then managed to scramble back upright. She clung on tightly with her knees but this only encouraged Luna to start trotting towards the field at high speed, Jessie bouncing on his back and desperately grabbing at his mane.

He bucked and leaped like a rodeo horse and each time he landed with a jolt against the ground, Jessie felt herself slipping further and further, until, with one final cat leap, she tumbled from his back and hit the ground hard. She felt the breath knocked out of her lungs and Luna took off across the field at top speed, bucking and leaping, eyes wide and nostrils flared like an Arabian stallion.

The two boys had been watching everything. Even in her dazed and confused state, Jessie wondered whether they had realised that it was her who had been riding Luna. However, through the dusty haze, she could see that the boys had dropped down from the wall and were running as fast as they could in the opposite direction. Jessie flopped back to the ground, her arm ached and she realised that Matthew, surely, could not have recognised her. Even though they did not get on most of the time, surely he wouldn't be so heartless as to run away when she was hurt?

"Jessie! Jessie!" Helen had seen what had happened and came running over. "Are you alright, love?"

***

Jessie knew that it was not really Luna's fault. That it had been the boys who had spooked him. She tried to remember the way it had felt to be sitting on his back, how calm and steady he had been, yet, there was a part of Jessie who felt let down by Luna. She had reached out to him, trusted him to look after her. Jessie's arm ached and she clutched it tightly against her ribs as Helen's car bounced through the potholes on the lane that led down into the village. Jack sat in the front passenger seat and looked out of the windows at the huge expanse of sea, glittering and vast as they traced the coastline in the little red car.

"Let me take you inside," Helen said as she pulled up outside Rose Cottage, but Jessie was already opening the door and halfway out, hoping that her mum had not been watching from the house.

"It's okay. Thank you for the lift."

The garden gate opened with a creak and Jessie trudged up the path. Indoors, her brother was rummaging in the kitchen cupboards. He spun around with a guilty look, clutching a packet of crisps, but relaxed when he realised it was only Jessie.

"Where's Mum?" she asked

"Out the back. Where were you today?" he asked, quickly stuffing the crisps into his mouth.

"Nowhere."

"So you weren't riding the white horse that belongs to the crazy old man, then?"

"What? No!"

Matthew walked up to Jessie and studied her face to try and work out if she was telling the truth.

"Hmm... Well, I'll be keeping an eye on you from now on."

Jessie scurried upstairs into the bathroom where she peeled off her sweatshirt and examined the dark bruise, which was spreading across her elbow. The pain had slowed to a dull ache. She washed her face with cold water to stop the tears that were welling in her eyes and took a deep breath. She had a choice, she could either stop going up to the Chalke's farm and never see Luna again, or she could take a risk. She would have to be careful, she might get caught. Her brother was definitely suspicious now, but it would all be worth it. Those few seconds on Luna's back made Jessie realise what was possible and she knew that with a little more time and effort, she could have everything that she had ever wanted.

With a decision made, she wiped her eyes, and felt stronger. It didn't matter what her brother thought or suspected. It didn't matter if she was keeping secrets from her mum. All that mattered was Luna and those precious few seconds when he had put all his trust in her.

Chapter 10

Autumn seemed to appear all of a sudden that year. Jessie woke up one morning and noticed that the air felt different. Autumn changed the colour of the light, made the brittle leaves on the trees rattle, painted long dark shadows on the hills. The swallows seemed to have noticed the changing seasons too, lining up along the telegraph wires, preening and chirping, getting ready to disappear over the sea to a warmer winter. The waves had darkened from tropical blue to a harder, steel-grey. The breeze became a little stronger, splashing flecks of foam onto the cliffs and tossing seagulls higher into the air.

With only a couple of days left of the summer holidays, autumn brought with it a hundred memories. Gone were the long, hot summer days of adventures and secrets and horses. One deep breath of autumn made Jessie think of bowls of porridge, socks drying on the radiator, a flickery electric light on cold floor tiles. Memories of her dad seemed to shine brighter amongst the dim autumn colours, no longer dazzled by summer; memories of him tying her shoelaces and tucking her scarf inside her coat, waking her up when it was still dark outside and cutting the crusts off her sandwiches for her packed lunch. She thought of him far more now, as her mum dragged them through high streets to find school uniforms and sat in cafes as the rain pattered against the window.

With all the preparations for school, there had been less time to spend with Lauren and the ponies; knowing that the carefree days of Summer were coming to an end, soon to be replaced by dark nights and school days, Jessie spent the final precious moments with Luna and, the day before the new school year started, Jessie made one last visit to the hut.

She hadn't been up to the hut for some time but everything looked just the same as before. The same garden chairs, although one lay on its side now, knocked over by the wind. The same crate, which was used for a table. The same collection of biscuit wrappers and mugs and the old barbecue. The wind rattled the roof and whistled through the gaps and holes. Jessie peeped inside and, there, on the wooden crate, was another white envelope. Jessie opened it and, inside was a new photograph. When her eyes had adjusted to the dim light, she gasped with surprise. The photograph was of Luna and a girl. It must have been taken a few weeks ago as the sky was very blue. Luna held his head low and relaxed, his eyes closed as if he had fallen asleep. The girl was just a dark silhouette sitting on the fence beside him. To anybody else it would have been impossible to tell who this person was; their features were in shadow. However, on looking a little closer, Jessie knew that it could only have been herself.

***

The first day at her new school dawned bright and sunny. She sat on the ledge that framed her bedroom window in her pyjamas and could see the moorland ponies grazing. She had forgotten about them a little over the summer, when the excitement of riding had taken up so many of her thoughts. They had been there the whole time, of course and, that particular morning, they seemed to represent everything that was being taken away from Jessie with the start of school - freedom, open skies and the great outdoors. She should be out there, racing across the grass in her shorts and t-shirt, hair tangled and sun on her skin, not in here getting dressed into the new, stiff and uncomfortable uniform her mum had grabbed from the supermarket shelf in a panic a couple of days ago. She glared at the spot where the uniform hung on her wardrobe door.

"Come on, Jessie!" her mum yelled from downstairs "Get yourself dressed now or you'll miss the bus!"

Jessie groaned and slowly slid off the window sill. She got dressed and pulled the photo out from its hiding place in the drawer under her bed. She looked again at the picture of herself and Luna. It didn't seem real. She wondered if she should show Lauren the picture or not. It was impossible to see that Jessie was the girl in the photograph but it was still a risk. Perhaps Lauren would put two and two together and guess what Jessie had been up to all summer. Yet, to keep this one, final photo, the last remnant of their summer adventure from Lauren, felt like a betrayal of her trust. She tucked the picture into her school bag and looked forward to lunchtime when she would find Lauren and show it to her.

***

Four hours later, Jessie had sat through three dull lessons, met Alice - a tall prefect with braces on her teeth, been given six exercise books and got lost twice. Alice had shown Jessie to the canteen where the raucous chatter of children and scrape of chairs echoed through the hall. After the summer she had just spent alone on the moors, or galloping free with only Lauren by her side, the noise and the choking smells of meat and vinegar and custard was overwhelming. The floor was sticky with spilt drinks and Jessie side-stepped the splatter of mashed potato carefully. She wanted to run outside, where the air was fresh and clean, she would much rather have mud on her shoes than the remains of somebody's school dinner.

As Jessie and Alice waited in the queue for lunch, Jessie spotted Lauren pushing her way through the heavy doors, surrounded by a giggling group of girls. Jessie was surprised at the wave of relief that she felt on seeing a familiar face.

"Can I just go and talk to my friend?" she asked Alice.

"Of course! You're free to do what you like at lunchtime. I'll meet you at the bottom of the stairs by reception in 25 minutes to take you to your next lesson, that okay?"

Jessie nodded and left the queue to catch Lauren before they disappeared into the crowds of children.

"Hiya!" She shouted over the noise of clattering dishes and chattering voices.

The group of girls that Lauren was with turned and looked Jessie up and down, making her feel awkward and uncomfortable. She felt like a moth trapped in a jam jar, being stared at by unfriendly strangers.

"Oh, hi Jessie," Lauren smiled.

"Hi, I've got something..." she started excitedly, reaching into her pocket, fingers closing on the photo inside.

"Not another pic from our friendly ghost, is it?" Lauren smirked and the other girls laughed loudly.

"What's this, Lauren?" One of them asked.

"Oh, just a silly thing Jessie and I did over the summer. There was a hut, and some photos and Jess thought that they were being taken by a ghost!"

"You thought that, not me," Jessie bit back but Lauren had turned and was already laughing with the rest of the girls. As they walked away, Lauren glanced back at Jessie with a look which seemed to say *'sorry, but things are different at school.'*

Jessie felt embarrassed. Her fingers tightened on the crumpled picture in her pocket. Embarrassment turning   to   anger.

***

When they got off the bus and Jessie turned to go home, Lauren appeared beside her and put a hand on her shoulder.

"Did you say you wanted to show me something earlier, Jess?" She asked, interested again now that her other friends weren't around.

"No, it was nothing."

"Don't be like that, Jess. You're not upset about earlier are you?"

"Course not," Jessie shrugged and started to walk towards home.

"Aren't you coming to the yard?"

"Not today. See you later." Jessie smiled sadly.

She had intended going straight home; to answer the hundred questions her mum would fire at her, to change out of her school uniform and to eat her tea, however, as she neared the little gate which led out to Luna, the desire to see him was too strong. Glancing around to make sure nobody was watching, Jessie dashed through the gate. Her bag was too heavy, full of all the new books she had been given that day, so she tucked it away in a big patch of bracken, making sure it was well hidden, before making her way over to Helen and Jack's farm.

As she walked through the dusty yard in her new school shoes, she could see Luna and Bob grazing, the sun shining on their backs. As she neared the gate, both horses heads shot up to look at her and Luna let out a soft, gentle whicker in greeting. Jessie felt her heart skip a beat. She could have cried. All summer she had wanted to hear that noise; some kind of recognition, a connection between them. She climbed over the gate and half walked-half ran over to Luna who stood calmly as Jessie wrapped her arms around his neck and nuzzled her face into his sleek white coat. She only let go when she felt Bob's whiskery muzzle poking about in her pockets, searching for carrots. She giggled and turned to Bob kissing his face and stroking his coarse mane.

"What are you doing up here in your school uniform, young lady?" Helen asked in a stern voice. Jessie smiled sheepishly.

"I won't be long."

"Your mum will be wanting to know how your first day went."

"I just wanted to see Luna first."

"It wasn't too bad, was it?"

"It was alright." Jessie had already forgotten about most of the day. Luna's whickered greeting had wiped all other thoughts from her mind.

***

Jessie walked home, remembering to stop at the patch of bracken where she had left her school bag. However, as she pushed aside the ferny leaves, it was gone. There was a slightly flattened space where the bag had once been but no sign of it at all. Perhaps somebody had seen her put it there and gone back to take it, but who would want to steal a schoolbag? There had been nothing valuable inside. Fear gripped Jessie's stomach. She frantically looked under every bush and amongst the long grass in the hopes that whoever had taken it had realised it was not worth anything and thrown it away. In the end she realised that she would have to go home without it. As she walked back up the road, she tried to think of an excuse that her mum would believe. She thought about tomorrow, having to tell all her new teachers that she had lost the things they had given her already. The thought of their harsh words and disapproving looks made Jessie feel sick.

She got through the door and knelt down on the cold floor to unlace her shoes when her brother appeared at the foot of the stairs. The light was dim and Jessie's eyes were still adjusting from the brightness of outdoors. Her brother's figure was shadowy but when Jessie looked up at him she could see a smile on his face. He reached for something behind his back and held it out in front of him. It was her schoolbag.

"Been looking for this?" he asked.

Chapter 11

"Give me that!" Jessie lunged towards her brother, trying to grab the bag. Her brother laughed and jumped backwards up a couple of stairs.

"What have you got in here that you want to hide?" he asked, unzipping the bag and pulling out a couple of books. The white envelope containing the photograph of Luna fluttered to the floor like a feather. Jessie grabbed at it and kept it clenched tight in her fingers.

"What is that?" Matthew asked, his eyes twinkling with excitement, "A love letter! Jessie's got a boyfriend, Jessie's got a boyfriend!"

He hopped up and down on the stairs.

"What's going on?" Their mum appeared from the kitchen.

"Jessie's got a note that she doesn't want anyone to see. It's a love letter."

"No, of course it isn't!" Jessie screamed.

"What is it then, Jess? And where have you been? I was expecting you home ages ago."

"It's just a note that Lauren gave to me. Asking me to help her at the yard after school."

"And that's where you've been all this time? At the yard?

"Yes!" Jessie cried.

"Okay, well, Matthew give your sister her bag back. And Jessie, you are not to go to the yard after school any more. It's weekends only from now on."

Jessie snatched her bag off Matthew and barged past him on the stairs. She flung her bag across her bedroom and stuffed the envelope in her pocket. Just as she was about to close her bedroom door, Matthew appeared in the doorway. He paused and grinned.

"I saw you hide your bag earlier and I know that you weren't going in the direction of the stables," he said quietly, "I'm not sure what you were up to but I'll bet it has something to do with that white horse."

He quietly stalked away and Jessie slammed the door shut behind him.

The weeks passed slowly. September turning into October. The days getting shorter, the nights longer. The time between weekends seemed to pass so slowly and yet the hours that she was at the Chalke's farm passed by in a blur. The autumn had brought the rain with it, and the field that Luna and Bob had shared all summer was already turning to mud. Helen had decided to keep them both stabled for most of the time, only allowing them out onto the concrete yard for a few hours each day.

Jessie already noticed the difference in Luna. He had gone from being calm and relaxed to tense, unpredictable. Jessie was nervous to be in the stable with him as he was likely to swing around suddenly or barge past her to escape. One day, Jessie had noticed Jack sitting in his chair by the window. He had a sad look on his face as he watched her through the glass. She turned and saw Luna had the same expression on *his* face as he poked his head over the stable door. Jessie felt sure that Jack would keep Luna differently if he were able to.

Most of the time spent at the riding stables was also spent doing indoors jobs; cleaning the green mould that quickly formed on the saddles in the tack room, mucking out stables, filling endless hay-nets. When they rode, it was always in the indoor school where the instructor's voice echoed loudly and the horses' breaths formed a misty cloud about their heads. Jessie longed for the summer to return; to walk on the moors, to swim in the sea, to ride through the fields.

In the evenings, when she was meant to be doing her homework, Jessie would often clamber up onto the ledge by her bedroom window. She would wrap herself in a blanket and look outside into the darkening gloom to see if she could spot the wild ponies that she knew were out there somewhere. Jessie liked this moment of calm as the sun was setting and the dim light turned her bedroom blue. The rain pattering against the windows, the wind howling contrasted with the homely sounds of cutlery rattling and the smell of dinner cooking, which drifted up the stairs.

It was in moments like this, when Jessie couldn't imagine being anywhere else, that her thoughts would often turn to her dad. She spoke to him once a week on the phone, told him about Cornwall, about the ponies at the stables. But, in the quiet moments, as she sat at her window, he felt so distant, as though he were drifting away, becoming a part of a different life.

She imagined him in a darkened room, unshaven face lit by the flickering TV screen as he ate his lonely dinner. Or maybe not, maybe he had a new girlfriend now. Maybe she had kids. Maybe he was picking up their toys and reading them stories.

"Dinner's ready!" the call came from downstairs and Jessie would slide down from the window ledge and return to the warm yellow light, the dinner on the table and the rest of her family squabbling and arguing.

***

It had been nearly a month since Jessie had last visited the hut. The thought of her brother keeping an eye on her every move had made her nervous. Besides, that little hut that had seemed so peaceful and friendly in the summer had changed in Jessie's mind now. When she pictured it now it was bleak and grey, washed the same colour as the rain and the sea. The thought of it clinging to the rocks as the winds howled made Jessie feel lonely but, with thoughts of her dad on her mind and ideas that the mysterious stranger, who she had felt so intrigued by all summer, was also alone, Jessie decided to return to the hut once more.

The next Saturday morning, the rain had stopped and the thick grey clouds hung heavy over the moors. The mossy moorland turf had soaked up the water like a sponge. Jessie put on some wellies and a raincoat and headed out just as the streetlights were switching off. She traipsed across the moors with the hood of her sweatshirt pulled up to keep her ears warm.

The walk felt longer than it had in the summer. It was harder going with boggy patches to avoid and the strong wind pushed against Jessie as she tried to walk into it. Above Helen and Jack's land, she paused for a moment, trying to make out Luna's nose poking out of his stable, hoping that she wouldn't hear him crashing about inside. Nothing. There was no sight nor sound of him. Jessie would go to see him later.

As she reached the brow of the hill above the lake she stopped to watch the ripples of the water and the way they reflected the grey sky. She also saw the dark figure of a person by the lake's edge. That must be them! Jessie thought. The person who she had seen just the one time, with the sun in her eyes and the bright glare of light on the lake. The person who had left all of those photos all summer. Aware that any noise might make the person run again, Jessie very quietly descended the slope, placing each foot carefully to avoid dislodging the loose stones. She zig-zagged her way to the bottom.

The person was female. She had long red hair and wore a thick woolly jumper, a pair of jeans and walking boots. It was hard to tell her age; older than Jessie but younger than her mum. She was crouching down beside the lake's edge with a camera in her hands. Following the direction of the camera lens, Jessie

~ 103 ~

realised that she was taking photos of the moorland ponies. She was so focussed on getting a good shot that the girl did not notice Jessie standing beside her until she was only a few metres away. She spoke without even looking up from her camera.

"I wondered how long it would take you to find me," she said in a calm, quiet voice.

Jessie stayed quiet, not knowing what to say to this stranger. When no answer came, the girl looked up and seemed surprised to see Jessie standing there.

"Oh, sorry!" she said, flustered and standing up quickly, stumbling and nearly falling into the lake "I thought you were someone else."

Jessie felt awkward, those photos had been meant for another person. She looked down at her feet and started to walk away.

"Hang on a minute!" the girl called out "I recognise you. I know your face."

How could she possibly know her. Jessie had never seen this person before in her life.

"Come here a minute, let me show you something."

Jessie walked over and the girl pressed some buttons on her camera and showed the screen to Jessie.

"Look. These are the pictures I've been taking all summer."

Jessie crouched next to the girl and saw the beautiful photo she had just taken moments before of the moorland ponies looking out across the lake. The girl flicked backwards through the pictures. Most of the pictures were of the herd of ponies, different settings, different weather conditions but the same seven ponies who Jessie had spent so long watching herself.

"You know these ponies too, don't you?" she asked. Jessie nodded her head. "You have watched them as much as I have."

She kept moving backwards through the pictures and the autumn changed back to summer. And then there was another picture. A picture of Jessie herself standing beside Luna. The lead rope slack in her hands and his head dropped down to the level of Jessie's head. The girl paused on this picture and turned to look at Jessie closely.

"This is you, right?" she asked.

"Yeah."

"And you are looking after Luna."

Jessie turned, how did this girl know his name?

"I'm Anna," she smiled. Her face was pale and her eyes nervous. She bit her lip anxiously.

"Anna? I've seen a picture of *you*. Jumping Luna at a show."

"How is he? My old boy."

Jessie thought of him standing alone in his stable. Nibbling on a strand of hay and flinching suddenly at the slightest creak or rattle.

"He doesn't like being in his stable."

Anna shook her head.

"No, I shouldn't imagine he does."

Jessie wanted to ask Anna a hundred questions; about Luna, about Jack and Helen, about how she could get Luna to trust her enough to let him ride her, but Anna had stopped talking and moved a few paces away. She still watched the moorland ponies who were gathered together resting, flicking an ear now and then at the sound of a gull or the splashing of waves. The moment for questions seemed to have passed now.

"I'm going to see Luna now, will you come with me?" Jessie asked. Anna's back was still to her and she did not turn around but answered.

"I don't think I can. It's better that he has you now."

Anna sat on the ground at the lake's edge. She pulled out a cloth and began cleaning the camera's lens. Jessie stood beside her, fidgeting with the sleeves of her sweatshirt nervously.

"I wish I could ride Luna like you used to," she blurted out.

Anna turned to look at her.

"I wish I had known more back then. I never would have ridden him like I did."

"Why?"

"Because it was wrong. Hey, look at those ponies," she pointed at the herd who were resting at the lake's edge "do, you think that those ponies really want to be ridden? Want to be whipped and kicked and yanked in the mouth?"

Jessie looked at the ponies, they were so peaceful, so much a part of this natural landscape that she could never imagine them locked in a stable or cantering around a school.

"No."

"No. Of course they don't. Those ponies could so easily have been born into another life. One where they were passed onto a new home as soon as they had been outgrown. Having to fit into a new herd every few years. Having to form new bonds and try to understand what their new owners want from them."

One of the ponies ambled a little too close to its neighbour, who showed its annoyance by swinging its head around and pinning its ears back. The pony moved on, edging up to another, friendlier individual who was happy to start a mutual grooming session.

"They understand each other so completely. Every little move. Every twitch of an ear or the way they angle their bodies - it all means something. Horses as a species have survived thousands of years perfectly well without the help of humans. They don't need rugs to keep them warm in the winter, or a bucketful of oats every night. The reason they have survived is because of each other. Their little herd. *That* is the most important thing to a horse."

Jessie sat down beside Anna and listened to her talk sadly. The thought of those ponies living anywhere other than this little patch of moorland seemed so unnatural and wrong. Yet, there was also a part of Jessie that couldn't imagine only ever watching horses from afar, never touching them or grooming them or riding them.

"But, can't we become their friends? Can't we teach them to trust us?"

"I used to think that once. I used to think that Luna and I would never be separated. That he loved me as much as I loved him. But now, I don't know. I think that he would have been just as happy wandering about on the moors, like these ponies, as he was being groomed and fussed over by me."

"I just want him to be happy."

Anna looked at Jessie and her face softened.

"I know. I could see that even through my camera when I took your picture back in the summer. And it is for you to decide what the right thing to do is. It doesn't matter what anyone else tells you."

"I want to learn though. I want to know as much about horses as I can. I want to know how to take care of them and give them everything they need."

"Even Uncle Jack would tell you that you can learn as much about horses from watching these ponies as you can from any riding instructor."

"I wish I had known Jack before he got sick."

Anna turned, startled.

"Sick?"

"Well. Maybe not sick; old and forgetful. Most of the time it's like he is somewhere else."

Anna picked up a stick and began poking about in the sandy earth. She bit her bottom lip and didn't look up.

"You did know?"

"No," Anna said quietly, "I haven't seen him for so long."

Chapter 12

"Do you think horses like being ridden?" Jessie asked Lauren as they walked through the canteen with their lunches on trays, squeezing past pupils until they found a free table.

"Yeah, course they do," Lauren answered, shovelling a forkful of mashed potato into her mouth, "Why would you ask that?"

Jessie shrugged her shoulders and pushed her lunch around on the plate.

"I just wondered. I thought it might hurt them."

"Well, you don't have to hurt them. They learn to respond to just a little squeeze with your legs and a gentle feel on the reins."

Jessie thought about the riding stables and the whips and the loud voices. There was nothing gentle about the way some of those people rode.

"And anyway," Lauren continued, "sometimes you have to be firm. You have to be the leader so the horse does what you want."

"Yeah, I guess," Jessie said, thinking of the slight changes of body language, the smallest flick of an ear or wrinkle of a nostril, that meant leadership to the moorland ponies.

"Do you want to come for a ride with me tomorrow? Nathan is away on a school trip for the weekend so you could ride Star."

So that explained why Lauren had bounced up to her at the beginning of lunchtime, then, Jessie thought. She usually kept her distance at school to avoid the girls who always surrounded Lauren. Instead she had found her own friends. Yet, today, Lauren had caught up with her in the lunch queue and started chatting happily. It must have been because she needed a friend to ride with at the weekend. Still, it would be nice to be able to ride again. After that initial couple of seconds on Luna's back, she was starting to lose hope that she would ever be able to ride him properly.

"Yeah, okay," Jessie said, smiling as she started to eat her yoghurt.

***

It was good to be riding again. Being outdoors on Star's back as they trotted across the spongy grass, the glittering sea reflecting the sky, it brought back memories of the freedom of summer. Only, instead of blue and turquoise, the sea and sky were the same steel grey. The clouds patterned with black like a mackerel's skin. The air tasted rainy and there was something a little wild and unpredictable about the way the breeze would suddenly gather strength, jostling and buffeting against the ponies' sides before quietening down to a whisper.

Star bounced along behind Lauren and Charlie. Jessie sat quietly. She felt as though any slight movement would encourage Star into a wild gallop from which she would not be able to stop. Her mane danced in the wind and her ears were pricked. After the last few weeks of riding lessons, Jessie felt nervous again to be riding out across the open moorland. She clutched the reins and when Lauren wasn't looking, she let her hands drift across to hold onto the front of the saddle. Lauren turned around and grinned.

"Isn't this great?" she shouted over the sound of the wind and the waves.

"Yeah," Jessie smiled, "Great!"

"Just relax. Star won't do anything silly."

A flock of jackdaws clattered through the skies before dropping into the treetops where they began cawing loudly. Star leapt sideways and Jessie snatched at the loose reins, hauling herself back into the saddle and clinging on tightly. Charlie calmly plodded on ahead. His thick tail swishing from side to side and Jessie could just make out a faint tune that Lauren was quietly singing. They were nearing the fork in the path where one track led to Luna, the other to the hut by the lake and the route they would take to go back to the stables. Jessie looked down and could see Luna and Bob out in the yard, their stable doors were tied back and they were sharing a hay-net.

"Look!" Lauren pointed in the direction that Jessie was looking, "the horses are out! Let's go down to see them."

Jessie panicked.

"No! No! Come on, let's go this way."

"Why? Come on, Jess. We can just ride along the bridleway for a quick look."

Jessie could imagine it all. Jack sitting by the window. Luna spotting the ponies. His hooves clattering on the concrete. Jack tapping on the glass. Helen coming outside to see what the fuss was all about. Seeing Jessie. Calling to Jessie. The secret over.

"No. Come on Lauren. We need to keep going this way. Look, it's starting to rain, we should get back."

The first fat drops of rain were spotting Jessie's coat but Lauren was already turning down the path, heading in the direction of the barn. Jessie closed her fingers on the reins and held Star back for a few moments, hoping to wait until Lauren returned. However, Star stamped her hooves, tossed her head and exploded forward in a fast trot to catch up with Charlie.

They neared the yard and Luna's head shot up when he noticed the ponies. His nostrils flared as he let out a shrill whinny and took a few steps closer. The girls continued to ride along the bridlepath as it led alongside the paddock. The ground was stony and the hedges thick with brambles, Jessie had to duck underneath overhanging branches as the path narrowed. Luna was standing pressed up against the field gate, whinnying loudly.

"Come on, we can't go any further," Jessie urged.

"Just a little closer," Lauren replied, "we can get a better look if we just go down here."

Star pranced and tossed her head. Jessie closed her eyes and gripped the reins tightly. Luna whinnied again and, finally, with one huge leap, launching himself from a standstill, he scrambled over the gate. In moments, he was gone, away, galloping across the field. He passed the place where the ponies were standing and whinnied as his hooves sped over the short grass.

Star screamed a shrill whinny in response and, quick as lightning, she spun around on her hind feet and pulled the reins through Jessie's fingers. She was off, hooves clattering on the stones and leaves and brambles whipping against her sides. The sky and the trees turned into one grey blur and the rain stung Jessie's face as they galloped along the path.

"Jessie!" Lauren yelled, her voice thin as the wind whistled in Jessie's ears.

She clung to the front of the saddle as Star slipped and leapt over the stones. She leant low over Star's neck and closed her eyes, hoping that the overhanging branches would not knock her out of the saddle. The track widened and the trees thinned as Jessie saw that the open moorland was quickly approaching. Luna was nearing the hedge that separated his field from the moors. The hedge was no higher than the gate that he had just jumped and Jessie knew that he would not have too much trouble clearing it if he really wanted to.

Star, taking a shorter route, reached the moors moments before Luna. She slowed to a trot for a few strides and Jessie tried to gather her reins with numb, trembling fingers. But just as she thought that she was regaining some control, she looked to the side, pushed her dripping fringe away from her eyes and saw Luna leaping in a perfect arc over the hedge. His mane splayed in the air, his knees tucked under his chin, his hind legs stretched out behind him. In that split second, Jessie remembered the photograph of Luna and Anna.

Then, they were off again. Luna and Star galloping across the moors, side by side. Jessie clinging to the saddle, gripping with her knees as she tried desperately to stay on. Star's breathing was loud as she bolted across the grass. She could hear Luna's pounding hooves. If she could have watched herself from a distance, Jessie would have felt exhilarated, excited to be so close to Luna at his most beautiful and powerful. She could have imagined that she were sitting on his back and could feel his mane brushing her fingers.

However, Jessie felt nothing but terror. She tried in vain to pull on Star's reins but they had slipped through her fingers again and Star wasn't listening. The seconds felt like hours. And suddenly, Jessie looked up. Like an angel standing amongst the rocks, her figure silhouetted against the sky, her long hair dancing in the breeze, Jessie saw Anna. She had started to run, hurtling down the slope, leaping nimbly amongst the boulders. Luna and Star were tiring now and Star seemed to have realised that Charlie was missing. She called loudly and an answering whinny echoed from back by the field.

"Jessie!" Anna called as she half ran, half stumbled down the slope to the spot where Star stood gasping for breath. "Jessie, are you okay?"

Jessie was shaking so much. She just wanted to get off Star's back but her legs felt wobbly. Anna grabbed hold of Star's reins and helped pull Jessie down from the saddle, her legs nearly buckled beneath her but she managed to prop herself against Star's shoulder. Anna handed Jessie the reins, her numb fingers refusing to curl around the straps, as Anna quickly began to unhook the stirrups from the saddle. She pulled the stirrup irons off the leathers and buckled the two leathers together.

"What are you doing?" Jessie asked, her voice shaky.

"Just wait there for two seconds."

She walked quietly over to Luna who stood with his sides heaving and neck arched proudly. She spoke to him softly and he seemed to know her immediately. He dropped his head and allowed Anna to rub the spot between his eyes. She looped the stirrup leathers around his neck and he trusted her enough to walk beside her back to Jessie.

"Come on. Let's get Luna put away and you back home again," she said. Jessie nodded and felt a lump tighten in her throat and chest. She wiped the tears from her cheeks and led Star along behind Luna.

Chapter 13

They walked back towards the house in nervous silence. Jessie's legs were wobbly and she kept herself upright by hanging onto Star. The outline of the farmhouse looked bleak against a backdrop of grey waves and dark sky. The rays of a low, autumn sun pierced through the thick blanket of clouds, acting like spotlights to bring a tree, a patch of ground, a seagull into sharp definition. Jessie felt as though she were on a stage and with each step nearer the house she could see the audience watching on. Helen, Jack and Lauren kept their eyes fixed on Anna and Jessie as they walked across the moorland under the dancing light.

One step after another. One wave breaking after another. The sound of the sand shifting, the pull of the tide. A deep breath in, a deep breath out. The familiar sounds now signalling some change that was about to happen. A change that Jessie had caused to happen. They reached each other at the field boundary and the stillness was broken by anxious chattering and fidgeting and shuffling. And then a silence. A pause in the conversation as Helen registered who this stranger was.

"Anna!" her voice wobbled and cracked, "it's been so long!" she exclaimed, stepping forward to try and wrap her arms around the young woman. Anna took a step back, her hands coming up to block the affectionate embrace and instead thrust the stirrup leathers that were looped around Luna's neck into Helen's hands. She looked down, away from Helen, but could not stop herself glancing quickly up at Jack who stood just behind her. He looked at her but did not know her. His eyes glazed over and he saw her only as another young woman in the stream of strangers who passed through his life; the cleaner, the lady who delivered the post, the woman who worked on the till in the supermarket. One after another, each as unrecognisable as the next, forgotten as soon as they had appeared. Her grown up features bore no resemblance to the childish ones that had been so cherished so many years before. They belonged to someone else now. A stranger.

"Sorry. I have to go," Anna murmured, before she set off walking, as quickly as she could, in the opposite direction; breaking into a run and then slowing to a fast walk again.

"Jessie, are you okay? What happened? Let's get Luna put away. Come on." Helen lead Luna down the path and let him run back to the yard where Bob was pacing anxiously up and down the fence.

Helen ushered Jessie and Lauren around the side of the house where they could let the ponies graze in the garden, between the buddleia and fuchsia bushes. Their girths were loosened, a knot tied in their reins and stirrups run up as Helen brought out cups of sugary tea for the girls to sip and even though Jessie usually hated tea when her mum made it for her, she instantly felt calmer as she drank it. They sat on the garden bench

~ 119 ~

beside a hydrangea bush covered in dead, brown flowers and a robin hopped about beneath pecking at worms. A few plant pots, freshly planted with bulbs that would explode with colour come the spring, lined the path. Inside the house, Jessie could see Jack through the misty, rain flecked window. He paced up and down, twisting his hands nervously.

"Is Jack okay?" she asked.

"He's just calming down. He gets confused and muddled so easily."

"Sorry."

"It's not your fault, is it? You weren't to know that Anna would suddenly appear like that."

"I knew that she was back."

"What? How?"

"I met her, a couple of weeks ago."

Jessie watched Lauren over the top of her mug. She looked quietly angry; Jessie could see her trying to fit pieces of the jigsaw puzzle together.

"She was the one who left the photos in the hut, wasn't she?" she asked, her voice quiet but hard.

Jessie nodded.

"You kept all this to yourself, didn't tell me about any of it."

"I'm sorry," Jessie whispered.

"Look, girls, it's all okay. Jessie, you can keep coming to help out with Luna. If you were worried that we'd suddenly stop you from seeing him then don't... it's okay, get yourselves home now and we'll see you again next weekend."

Lauren's face reddened with anger. As they caught their ponies and led them down the path towards the village, Lauren was silent.

"Wait!" a voice called to them from the house.

Jack was running down the path, his old legs wobbly but he was determined to catch up with them.

"Wait! Come back."

Jessie stopped and looked back at him, she felt sorry for him. He looked so vulnerable with his white hair unkempt and his walking stick. Jessie turned and waited.

"Anna? Where is she?"

"I don't know, Jack," Jessie murmured, letting her dark fringe hide the tears which were beginning to well in her eyes.

"We can't let her go again."

***

At school the next day, Jessie sat in the library during the lunch break. She didn't feel hungry. Her stomach was in knots and she anxiously chewed her fingernails as she stared at the words in her book without taking any in.

"You've been on the same page for the last twenty minutes," the librarian was sorting the books on the shelf behind her. "Anything wrong?" she asked, concerned.

"No," Jessie snapped and quickly turned to the next page.

She looked out of the window and watched the children playing outside. Even through the glass Jessie could hear their excited shrieks and bursts of laughter. She felt more lonely than ever. Lauren dashed by, followed by her usual group of friends. Seeming to sense she was being watched, she stopped in her tracks and looked straight at Jessie through the window, her face darkened and eyes glared at her before racing off again in a whirl of blonde hair and duffle coat.

The rest of the school day passed slowly and on the bus ride home, Jessie sat with her chin tucked into the collar of her coat and leant her head against the cold window. With every lurch of the bus as it rattled around the bends and with every jolt of her seat, Jessie felt more and more irritated. Her teeth bit at the inside of her bottom lip until she could taste the metallic tang of blood in her mouth.

As soon as the bus stopped, Jessie leapt up, grabbed her bag and raced down the aisle as quickly as she could.

"Wait!" Lauren shouted. Jessie turned around to see her friend coming towards her. She felt a warm rush of relief inside her chest.

"I'm sorry, Lauren," she tried to explain "I wanted to tell you. I was going to tell you. But, well, I was just worried about mum finding out and not letting me see Luna anymore."

"I won't say anything," Lauren said, coldly.

"Thank you! And, now that you know, maybe, perhaps you could come up and help me. You know so much more about horses than I do. Perhaps, if you were helping me, we could try riding him."

"No." Lauren gripped her bag and began to walk away. "No. We can't be friends. I won't tell on you to your mum but we won't see each other anymore."

Jessie ran the whole way home.

***

As her mum hurried about gathering plates and cutlery, Jessie felt that she could crack and crumble into a million tiny pieces and her mum would not even pause for a moment to wonder where she had gone. By the time her dad called for his weekly chat, everyone was lounging on the sofa, stuffed full of food and brainlessly watching some rubbish on the TV. Jessie took the phone and dashed up to her bedroom where she sat on her bed in the dark. The sound of the wind and rain battered against the windows and Jessie did not think she had ever felt quite so alone.

"Are you okay tonight, Jess?"

"Yeah."

"You sure? You're very quiet."

Just a little concern and Jessie felt the tears welling in her eyes and a lump filled her chest so tightly that she did not think she could get any words out.

"Sweetheart. What's the matter?"

"Dad, can you come and take me home?"

Chapter 14

Later that night, when she had calmed down and was snuggled up in bed reading her book, Jessie regretted those words to her father. The thought of going back to blocks of flats, busy roads and brick walls was unbearable. Living in a house where the only green she could see was a little patch of grass verge would be like being in a prison after the summer she had just had. The moors, the sea, the fields and woods - *they* were home now. She was so lucky to live here. Why did that question have to slip out of her mouth?

Despite the lashing rain and howling wind, Jessie dressed up warmly the next morning and let herself out of the house. She left her usual note on the kitchen table and slipped out quietly whilst the others were sleeping. If her dad were to come and collect her, Jessie wanted to soak up every moment of Cornwall. She wanted to go away with her lungs full of salty Cornish air and the black earth beneath her fingernails. She wanted to have a thousand memories of stunted trees, of banks of purple heather, of turquoise waves and soaring seagulls still in her mind. Then, when she was sitting in her concrete cell, looking down on rows of traffic, she would be able to close her eyes and look at all those memories as though she were flicking through a photograph album.

Jessie went down onto the beach. The memory of laughter and ice creams were so distant that Jessie could hardly believe it had ever been summer. She walked along the shoreline collecting pretty shells and pebbles, filling her pockets with mementoes. She wanted to remember everything but knew that she would soon forget. Only a month into autumn and the memory of swimmers in the sea and striped beach towels had long gone. Imagine how it would be when she were back living in a city again. All memory of fresh air and open space would soon be replaced by noise and tarmac.

As Jessie made her way back towards the path leading away from the beach, she noticed another person. A woman. She was doing the same as Jessie, collecting shells and things that had been washed up from the sea. Her long red hair streamed out from beneath the brim of her hat, which she clutched tightly to her head to stop it flying away.

"Anna!"

Anna wiped the rain from her eyes and squinted in the dim light.

"Jessie, hey! I thought I was the only mad person to come out here on a day like today. What are you doing out in the cold? Does your mum know you're here?" Jessie shook her head. "Do you want me to take you home?"

"My dad will be doing that soon enough," Jessie said, sadly.

"Your dad? I didn't know he lived down here."

"He doesn't."

"Come on. Let's go and sit in the dry for a bit and you can tell me all about it."

They made their way over to the cafe, stepped inside and closed the door against the wind that buffeted and howled. Inside, people were eating their breakfasts, the windows misted with condensation and the steam from hot drinks and the kitchen swirled in billows. It was warm and puddles of water leaked from umbrellas left by the door. The air smelt of coffee, toast, seaweed and wet dog. Whilst Anna was ordering, Jessie went and found a table by the window. She crossed her arms on the sticky plastic tablecloth and rested her head on top. She gazed out of the window at the waves and the black sky and a couple of dog walkers who battled against the wind, their dogs racing in crazy circles on the sand.

"What's up, hun?" Anna asked, returning with two mugs of hot chocolate and Jessie could not stop herself from telling Anna everything. About the lies, the secrets, about falling out with Lauren and about how her dad would surely be coming to take her home soon, and, even if he didn't, all the secrets would come tumbling out now and her mum was certain to send her back once she knew.

"Well, perhaps you should tell her first," Anna suggested "it would show her that you understood you'd done the wrong thing and were sorry about it. Your mum would know that, I'm sure. Even if she was angry at first, she would realise that you had made the right choice in the end."

"Perhaps," Jessie sighed, "but, Luna..."

***

They finished their drinks and started off again towards Rose Cottage. The rain was pouring from heavy grey clouds and they could hardly see where they were going as streams of rainwater gushed along the road. Through the sheets of rain that seemed to blur the grey landscape around them, they battled against the weather. Down the lane and past the parked cars, their jeans stuck to their legs and wet hair plastered across their faces. They passed the pub, lit from within as a cleaner scrubbed the bar and the landlord cleared away glasses. Past the row of four shops, the 'Open' signs showed on the doors but there was not a single person around to buy anything.

They started to walk up the hill, past the primary school where Matthew was the class clown; king of his year already. The school reminded Jessie of her own school. She imagined that she were sitting at her desk now, flickering electric lights bright on the whiteness of walls and paper. She imagined gazing out of the window in that white classroom and looking at herself as she was now; a sodden, dripping girl. The Jessie in the rain laughed out loud at the Jessie in the classroom. Who would want to be sitting in there as words danced across pages when she could be out here, with the rain and wind, shadows and light?

They walked on, past the terraced cottages where Jessie could peer in through windows and catch sight of socks drying on a radiator, a cat curled on an armchair and a pan of water boiling furiously on a hob. Children ran past one window and then appeared again in the next, racing madly around the lounge. Jessie and Anna watched them through the misty windows but the children were completely oblivious. In their bubble of warmth and television, they had not noticed the weather outside their window.

Finally, Jessie's street was in sight. The familiar red post box, the streetlights that lined the pavement and shone bright orange in the gloomy morning. The cars lined up along the curb. A familiar car parked outside her house. Her dad's. The lights were on in the house, filtering out through the blinds. Jessie tried to picture her dad, who she hadn't seen in months, sitting in the living room. The lamplight showing the lines on his face, his worried eyes. The way he was talking to her mum. The words they would be saying to each other. Accusing, angry, hurt. A knot tightened in Jessie's stomach when she thought about having to go inside. She felt like she couldn't breathe.

"I can't! Not yet!" she cried and started running back down the road, heading for the gateway which led out onto the moors.

"Jessie! Wait!" shouted Anna, running after her.

The moors were speckled with puddles, pools of water that reflected the grey light and looked like hundreds of little windows into some unknown world.

Jessie splashed through them and kept on running until she was so out of breath she had to stop.

"You're going to have to go back, Jess," Anna said, catching up with her.

"I don't want to!" Jessie snapped, angrily.

"But where else are you going to go?"

"I wish I didn't have a family. I wish I just had myself and my horses and nobody else to think about. I wish I was like you."

"You don't mean that. You don't want to be like me."

"I do."

"No. More than anything, I wish that I still had my family around me."

Jessie stood up straight and looked at Anna through her dripping fringe. Her face was numb with the cold and she could feel her whole body shivering, her teeth chattered together. She knew she was right, where else could she go? Slowly she turned and began the walk back towards the village. In the misty glow of streetlights and the yellow light seeping through kitchen windows, Jessie saw seven dark shapes walking in a line around the curve of a hill. The moorland ponies had emerged from their sheltering places and were heading off again on a trek where only they knew the destination. They walked purposefully, stopping just occasionally to nibble at a bush or some grass. Jessie stopped, leaving some distance so that she would not spook them and Anna stood beside her.

"The one in the lead," Anna said, "I call him Thorn. He's always the first to explore. He's brave and curious and he doesn't much like sheep. He always sees them off it they get too near. He is very attached to one that I call Apple. They groom each other often but Thorn always initiates it, which means that he is the more dominant of the two. Apple is more independent most of the time. She often strays further away from the others and sometimes does not notice that they have moved on until they have passed out of sight, then she gallops like the wind to catch up with them. Oak, Ash and Birch are the three youngsters, they are more playful than the others, you often see them play fighting together or barging into each other. They aren't so respectful of the rest of the herd members' space until a pony, usually Willow, bares their teeth or pins their ears. Then the three young ones drop back into line straight away again. Willow is an older mare, all the others respect her and she is always the one to move them on to the next place. And then the last one is Gorse, she keeps the peace."

"How can you tell them all apart?" Jessie asked, amazed.

"I've spent a lot of time watching them. There are some physical differences, but mostly it's their behaviour that identifies them. They are individuals as well as part of one herd. They react to things in different ways."

"I wish I could notice those things."

"Well, once you've got things sorted out at home, maybe you can come with me one day. We can take some photographs and you can learn more about horse behaviour."

"I'd like that."

"Come on," Anna said, tugging at Jessie's sleeve, "let's get you back home to face the music."

***

Back at the house, Jessie stood on the doorstep for a moment and took a deep breath. Slowly, quietly, she pushed open the door and stepped inside. Taking off her boots, she hung her dripping coat above the radiator and glanced at herself in the mirror. Her face was red and puffy from the wind and rain, her wet hair was plastered to her forehead. She tried to smooth it back and make herself look normal again. She walked through the hallway and into the kitchen, leaving wet footprints on the lino.

At the table, Jessie saw her Mum's face first, looking at her above a mug of tea. Then, she noticed the figure of a man, his back to her. She could recognise him from the familiar checked shirt he was wearing and the way his dark hair was thinning at the back of his head. He turned around and Jessie saw the face of her Dad. The one person she had missed so much over the past six months. And yet, she felt guilty that the first thought to pass through her mind was *'I don't want him here'*

"Hi Dad," she smiled shyly.

"Jessie!"

In a flash, her dad had leapt from his chair and crouched to the floor, his arms wrapped around her. Jessie thought of the shells and pebbles that were still in her coat pocket, drying above the radiator. She was glad she would still have those when he made her go away again.

Chapter 15

The following days felt so strange to Jessie with her Dad sleeping on the sofa. She had thought of him often since they had moved away yet he seemed a part of her old life. Thoughts of her dad were so bound up with the cars and mobile phones and concrete of living in the city that he just didn't seem to fit in down here. To walk sleepily into the sitting room and find her dad rolling up a sleeping bag and straightening the cushions felt so out of place. He tried his best to slot into their new life, but everything he attempted seemed awkward. He didn't know which cupboard the plates were kept in, he took the wrong path when they went for a walk to the beach. All of these little changes seemed to frustrate him more and more as each day passed.

To stop her parents from asking questions, Jessie told them that she had fallen out with Lauren; that was the reason why she had been so upset, why she can asked her dad to take her home. They seemed to accept this as a reason and neither of her parents pushed her for a decision on what should happen next. Jessie knew that she should have followed Anna's advice and told her parents all about Luna, but she could not quite bring herself to.

She had only seen Luna on a few occasions by the time Bonfire Night came around. Whilst her dad was gathering up the coats and her mum was trying to force boots onto Megan's kicking feet, Jessie sat on the arm of the sofa. Her stomach was in knots and she couldn't quite understand why she felt so nervous. Perhaps it was the thought of Luna, alone in his stable, panicking. Perhaps it was the cold tension that was simmering beneath the pretence that everything was fine between her mum and dad; the way her mum anxiously fiddled with her hair, or the way the muscle in her dad's jaw clenched tight at the slightest criticism. As Jessie sat on the sofa, she felt as though the room were getting gradually dimmer, the shadows creeping across the white walls, the light in the hall too bright, fluorescent, unnatural.

The whole family trooped down to the village playing field for the firework display where all of the villagers were gathered around a huge bonfire; the flames licked at the branches and the smoke billowed in grey clouds against the black night sky. Sparks flew up from the fire to dance amongst the stars. Jessie stamped her feet and tucked her hands into her pockets to keep warm as they waited for the fireworks to begin. The knot in her stomach, twisting and clenching, when she thought of Luna.

Rockets shrieked through the sky to explode in great clouds of yellow stars. Roman candles burst up from the ground spraying blue and green sparks into the black night. Smoke trails wound amongst the stars in the sky. Jessie turned to look at her sister, a hat and scarf wrapped around her ears so the noise would be muffled. Her wide blue eyes watched the magic that was all around her. Matthew stood a little way off with his friends; they all had arms folded and eyes glued to the fireworks. Her mum looked back at her and smiled gently and, when Jessie looked across to her dad, he drained the last of the beer in his can and gave her a wink.

"Pretty impressive, hey Jess?" he shouted above the noise.

Jessie smiled and nodded but somebody else had caught her eye. Standing beside the bonfire, bundled up in a thick coat but with her long hair flickering bright red in the light of the flames, Anna watched the fireworks intently.

"Your dad hasn't taken you home then?" she asked.

"Not yet," Jessie replied, "I haven't told them about Luna yet, though."

"Oh, Jessie!" Anna exclaimed.

"What? I can't! Look."

When they looked back to where Jessie had been standing moments before, they could see the figures of her parents. Their bodies were black shadows against the flames and it was clear they were in the middle of a raging argument. Her mum's arms flailed against the orange fire, gesturing wildly and she could almost make out her father's loud voice above the shriek of the rockets. Jessie felt a mix of embarrassment, anger and fear as a firework lit up the strained faces of her parents; their black eyes flashing, lines on their faces drawn. The firework faded into the night and all was dark again for a moment, only to be followed by the next flash of light, which showed her mum angrily turning away with folded arms, bending down to where Megan was screaming from her pushchair.

"I can't stand it." Jessie felt her blood run cold in her veins. "Can we just go."

"Where?"

"To see Luna."

"Come on."

***

It was cold at the stables, their breath billowed in icy clouds around their heads as they trudged across the grass, which was already crisp with frost. The air smelt sharp and smoky. Luna was standing at the back of his stable, his head was low and Jessie thought for a moment that he was asleep. She cautiously approached the door and could see that his eyes were open. Wide open and ringed with white. He looked scared. His coat was dripping with sweat and his eyes had a dullness to them that made him look completely shut down, as though he had given up all hope. Jessie let herself into his stable and he did not even try to rush though the gap. She sat down in the corner nearest the door and took off her wet coat.

"I wish you could stay outside. If only you were my horse. I would never keep you in a stable. You could be out in the fields with Bob all day every day. I'd never do anything to frighten you. I'd just look after you, forever, never want anything more than that. I wish you'd just trust me," she murmured.

Anna followed Jessie inside and stood in the corner. Luna snorted with surprise but remained standing where he was. Anna smoothed her wild hair away from her face.

"Hey, boy. It's been a while," she soothed. Luna remained standing at the back of the stable. He allowed Anna to move a little closer to him but he still showed no signs of recognising her voice.

"We used to be the best of pals, didn't we? Did all the competitions together. Went out camping that one time, remember? Me, you, Midnight and Susie Turner - camping in that field up on the moors that belonged to the crazy bloke with all the chickens. The rain came down so heavily that we spent one night in mum's little tent before we were so fed up that we all trudged home again through the mud."

Luna was so quiet he seemed to be listening.

"And that other time, when we went down onto the beach and swam in the sea. I remember how slippery your sides were - I nearly fell off. And then, that time when Uncle Jack took us both over to see mum in the hospital. We rode past her window and I remember seeing her pale face above the white sheets - she always looked so sad, yet when she saw you and I, with the sun on our faces and the blue sky beyond - it was the first time I saw her smile. Really smile. It was the most beautiful I'd ever seen her look."

Anna was nearly at Luna's head.

"And then. The last time..." Anna's voice trailed off. She shook her head as if trying to dislodge the memory that was clinging to the inside of her eyes.

Luna dropped his head, his brow resting against Anna's stomach. She reached up a hand to smooth the sweat-curled coat along his neck. They both stood quietly for just a moment yet Jessie thought she had never seen two beings so connected as these two were. For a few seconds, they were no longer human and horse but one creature, remembering together the best and the worst of times.

Jessie sat quietly in the corner, not wanting to disturb them. She felt a little sad that the bond she had built up with Luna over the summer was shared with Anna in an instant.

"Please tell me what happened."

Her words seemed to shake Anna out of the dream she had been in before and she came over and dropped to sit down in the straw beside Jessie. The lights in the stable were switched on but outside the sky was pitch black. It felt as though the world had ended and only this stable remained, cast out into space with the night surrounding them.

They did not notice that, actually, whilst they felt very alone, they were not. Had they peered out into the darkness, they would have noticed the gate creaking open. An old pair of slippers shuffling across the concrete. A dressing gown tie trailing on the ground. Jack walked unsteadily from stable to stable, peering inside each one until he reached Luna's where he stopped outside and leant against the wall.

"I was thirteen when Mum died," Anna began and Jessie listened quietly.

Jack listened too, a vague feeling of sadness, which he was not sure he understood.

"Everything hurt so much that day, and the day after, and the weeks that followed. I can't begin to describe how much I missed her, how much I still miss her now. My dad was Uncle Jack's brother."

Luke, the name came to Jack's mind in a moment. His brother's name. And a thousand memories from their childhood flooded his thoughts for a brief moment. Followed by memories of his brother as a man.

"He missed Mum too, of course, although I didn't see that at the time. I know, now, that he was just so scared that the rest of his life would fall apart that he did all he could to hold onto me. But my dad has never handled things in the right way. He should have given me time, kept everything as normal as possible, been there for me. But everything that he did just pushed me further away."

Jack, leaning against the cold wall, had hazy memories of screaming rows and bitter words.

"I wanted my old life back. So I spent more time up here, with the horses, with Uncle Jack and Aunty Helen. Dad hated that. He blamed them for stealing me away. He was angry and twisted up with grief. So one day..."

As Anna spoke Jessie could picture the scene in her mind. She could imagine the farm as it was then. Clean painted walls, horses in the fields, chickens rooting amongst the straw. She pictured Anna as a young girl, as she was in that photograph Helen and Jack had shown her; red hair, pale skin and fierce dark eyes. She thought of Jack and Helen as they would have been fifteen years ago; younger, darker hair, smoother skin.

Anna's dad. Jessie could not imagine what he looked like. Yet, in her mind's eye he appeared as a looming, black shadow. A faceless, nameless shape that marched up the garden path, blue tits and green finches scattering into the trees as he rapped hard on the front door. He had barged past Jack and Helen had darted up the stairs behind him, pleading with him to stop as he threw open the door to Anna's bedroom.

She had stood in front of the window, behind her the horses grazed in the paddocks and beyond them, the wild ponies followed each other across the moors.

"You're coming with me," Anna's dad had barked and grasped hold of her shoulder so tightly Anna squirmed to move away from the pain.

"No, I'm staying here!" she had shouted in his face but he had dragged her out of her room, past Helen in the doorway and down the stairs. Jack stood in the kitchen looking, sadly, out onto the garden.

"Uncle Jack, please," Anna had begged "please let me stay here with you." Her dad grabbed her coat off the hook and opened the door.

"Sorry Anna. You should be with your dad."

And that had been the last time Anna had seen her aunt and uncle until the other day.

"But what happened to Luna?" Jessie asked. The lighting in the stable cast dark shadows under Anna's eyes and outside the wind was howling through the trees.

"I don't know why he did it," Anna continued, "whether it was because he was trying to hurt to Jack. Or perhaps, in his own strange way, he was trying to give me something which would make me happy. But a few weeks later, when I was out at school, he went back to his brother's house. He parked a car and trailer up on the moors and walked down that footpath which you and your friend rode down before."

Jessie grimaced at the memory of that day, the mad gallop under overhanging trees, Luna leaping the gate, knees tucked, mane splayed.

"Dad was carrying a can of petrol and in his pocket was a box of matches."

Jessie thought of the flames from the bonfire down in the village. Thought of the silhouetted figures of her parents arguing in front of the angry orange colours.

"No," she gasped.

"The horses were all in the stables for the night. Dad threw open the doors and the horses streamed out into the dark fields, through the open gates into the moors beyond. When all of the others were free, Dad opened Luna's stable. I can imagine him crashing against the doors as all his friends left. I can't begin to imagine how scared he must have been; with Dad gripping his lead-rope, he led Luna out into the yard. They looked back at the hay barn. I can't understand what Dad was thinking; he knew how much Jack loved the stables and the horses - they were his life. But it didn't stop him dropping that match amongst the hay.

As the flames began to rip through the stables, Dad lead Luna out of the yard, up the path and into the waiting trailer. I was so happy to see Luna when Dad gave him to me that I didn't notice the smell of smoke in his mane or the way his eyes rolled with terror."

If Anna had not created such a vivid picture in Jessie's mind, or if Anna had not been so consumed with remembering the past, both might had noticed a grey head passing by the open stable door. Jack left his spot against the wall and, as the windswept leaves tumbled across the yard, Jack too made his way to the gate. It opened with a creak that only Luna noticed. His ears pricked and he looked out into the black night.

"We had a good couple of years after that," Anna continued, " Luna helped me to cope with my mum's death. But my dad just became more and more difficult to live with. I wanted to stay. For Luna. But by the evening of my 16th birthday, my bags were already packed. I had a bus ticket in my coat pocket and would spend the next decade travelling, working and taking photos. Living in caravans, tents, hotels. Working wherever I could find a job. But I had to come back in the end."

Jessie looked at Anna and thought that she could still see a scared girl hiding just beneath the skin and eyes and clothes of a grown woman. She realised that everybody had different things to cope with at different times in their life but that nothing lasts forever, time moves on and people change and grow as a result.

She looked at Luna and thought that he had been the one constant for both Anna and herself. A steady rock during times of trouble. A bright star that shone every night even on cloudy days. Jessie should not feel jealous that he was important to more than just herself. She should be glad that he had come into her life at this time. She felt stronger because she knew that he was here and she was here; in the same place at the same time. And even though everything might change tomorrow, for now, in this stable, on this day, she had known him.

"You really should go to see Helen and Jack," Jessie said, firmly, "none of this was their fault."

Anna looked surprised.

"You're right," she said, "of course you're right."

Chapter 16

"Anna! Jessie! Why are you two here at this time of night?" Helen said, sternly.

"Where's Uncle Jack?" Anna asked in a frantic cry, "the back door was open and the gate to the horses field!"

"What? He's in bed," said Helen, already dashing to the stairs to go and check.

"Quick, Anna, call the police," she said from the bedroom, "Jessie, you really need to go home now, we can't look after you now. I'll take you home in the car, just go and wait outside for a second."

"Please, no, I can help..."

"Wait by the car," Helen cried.

Anna turned her back to Jessie as she dialled 999. Jessie dropped her head and looked up at Helen from under her dark fringe.

"Okay," she said.

Jessie slipped out through the door and crunched down the gravel path towards the little red car parked against the hedge. She looked back up the garden towards the house. The yellow light spilled from the windows and Jessie could see Anna pass the phone to Helen. Helen paced from the kitchen into the living room, talking rapidly into the telephone. She stood behind Jack's chair, her fingers gripping at the fabric. Anna rummaged in the drawers for torches. Jessie stood beside the car for a moment.

She had intended waiting and doing as she was told for once but her feet started to move in a way that felt out of her control. She started to walk, slowly at first, then quicker and quicker until, before she knew it, she was running. Her arms were flailing and heart pounding. She paused for a second and looked back. *I've already gone too far now*, Jessie thought, *I might as well just keep going.*

She darted away from the road and up onto the moors, keeping to the low stone walls and hedges. She scrambled across the uneven ground, stumbling, crawling on hands and knees, crouching as she felt her way around boulders. The air smelt sharp with smoke and the cold made her nose and throat sore. Losing her footing and collapsing into a patch of bracken, Jessie looked back and could see the black silhouette of the Chalke's farm, the moonlit sea glittering beyond. She heard the slam of the front door and then the engine of Helen's car start up. Jessie watched as the headlights swept across the black landscape and she held her breath, crouching low, watching through the ferny leaves. She could only imagine how worried Helen must be feeling and tears spilt from her eyes as she sat alone in the darkness.

She needed to find the path that would lead her home, yet the moors were so unfamiliar to her now. She had come to know this place so well in the daytime but the night seemed to play tricks on her. It was difficult to make out any landmarks and the hills and dips in the ground made her feel completely disorientated. The further Jessie walked, as the lights from the house vanished from view and the sound of the sea seemed to come from all directions, Jessie realised she was completely lost. She could not see even the boulders in front of her and she frequently tripped and fell, her hands grazed by the sharp rocks and brambles that twined around her legs. It was hopeless. She could be going round and round in circles for all she knew and the realisation that she had no idea where she was made her legs turn to stone. Panic caused her breath come out in short, shuddery gasps and she dropped onto her knees in an attempt to calm herself down.

Just as she felt that all hope was lost, that she would be out here all night with the air growing colder, she noticed that the sky was beginning to clear. Jessie could make out a few faint stars. Then a glow of the moon. The soft whooshing sound of waves lapping and breaking seemed to get louder. And suddenly, the clouds parted and the moon shone through with an intense brightness. However, the clear view gave Jessie little comfort.

No, no, no, Jessie thought, *this can't be right.* For the moonlight sparkled on the waves just a short distance away, whereas her home was on the road heading inland. She was further away than she could even have imagined.

Jessie slumped down to the cold ground and started to cry. She would *have* to stay here all night and she had lost all track of time. She could have been walking for hours. Perhaps she was somewhere she did not know and she would never be able to find her way home again.

She lay on the cold ground and pressed her fingers into the moss.

"I'll tell them all the truth," she sobbed.

"I'll never lie again, I promise," she wailed.

And then a sound. It was strange, Jessie had not realised until that very moment that it would be so familiar. A sound that felt like home. It reminded her of her bedroom with its window sill and cosy duvet. It reminded her of a summer sat in the garden with a blackbird singing in the apple tree. It was the coconut scent of gorse. It was strange that a sound could conjure up such feelings of home. A home that Jessie had not realised was home until she heard that gentle sound.

The sound was that of one of the moorland ponies. A soft whicker. Thorn stood a short distance away. Starlight glittered in his eyes and lit up the thick curly strands of his coat, the rest of the ponies were dark shapes grazing and moving about slowly behind him. Jessie smiled and then laughed softly and then laughed more and more until tears began to stream down her cheeks. The relief flooded through her like a giant wave. Thorn had looked confused at this odd behaviour and slowly ambled back to the rest of the herd.

Jessie followed him. She recognised this place now. Under the moonlight, she could recognise the

~ 147 ~

curve of a path, a hawthorn bush. A stunted wind-bent tree which looked as though it were forever stuck in a gale, pointed away from the direction of the hut. Jessie walked over to it.

She knew that she would find him. For some reason it seemed like just the place that would mean something to Jack. In the same way that Luna had meant something to others before Jessie herself. The hut, too, had been a place of adventure for more than just herself and Lauren. As Jessie drew near she noticed a faint glow coming from the open doorway. She felt a little nervous as she inched closer and called out to Jack before she got too near.

"Jack? Jack, are you there?"

There was no answer for a moment. A moment which seemed five times as long in the darkness. The night had painted the scenery blues and blacks but Jessie's eyes had adjusted now and she could make out a shadowy figure peering out of the hut.

"That is you, isn't it?" she asked.

"Where are you, Anna?" Jack called, "Why am I here?"

Jessie wasn't sure whether to correct him or not. He sounded frightened and she did not want to confuse him even further.

"Yes, it's me. Don't worry. I'll take you home," Jessie walked quickly up to Jack and took hold of his old, wrinkled hand.

"I thought that we were meant to be coming out here to watch the seals," Jack said quietly. "It's the best time of year and the females sing like mermaids from the sea caves."

"Yes, but we can't see them in the night time, silly."

"No, oh, of course. You're right, Anna, we will have to wait until the morning."

"Yes, we'll wait until the morning and then we can come back here."

"Yes." Jessie tried to start walking but Jack remained planted to the spot. "Wait, I remember now why I came up here. It wasn't for the seals. Something bad has happened. Your dad. He's done something to my horses."

"It's okay," Jessie soothed, "it's okay. It's all over now. Luna's safe. And I'm going to look after him forever."

"No. We need to get back. Quickly."

Jack broke free of Jessie's arm and started off across the moor at a surprisingly quick speed. Jessie had to run to keep up.

"Jack, slow down."

He kept marching onwards but after a few minutes, Jessie realised that he had not turned down the right path which would lead to his own farm. He was heading towards the village.

"Jack, please slow down. You're going the wrong way."

But Jack continued on without saying a word. Jessie stumbled after him, tripping over hummocks of grass and suddenly splashing into unseen puddles. The lights of the town grew brighter as they neared. Jessie could hear voices and laughter as people made their way home from the fireworks. She could see groups of people, families, walking up the road.

"Jack, stop. We need to go the other way."

Then Jessie heard, in the distance, her own name being called. She looked in the direction of the sound and could see the beam of torchlight scanning across the moors. The small dark figure of her brother, gesturing in the direction of the path they were walking along. The taller dark shapes of her parents following.

"This way!" Matthew called, "I know she'll be with the horse!"

The secret was over. Jessie was surprised that the first feeling to hit her was relief. To have everything out in the open, to be able to tell her parents everything at last, she finally felt free of her guilty secret. But a second feeling of anxiety and nerves quickly replaced it as her family drew near.

"Mum! Dad! I'm over here," she cried.

"Jessie! Thank God," her mum wrapped her up in a hug and her dad stroked her hair.

"Who is this, Jess?" he asked, gesturing to Jack.

"Jack. He's missing. We need to take him home."

There was no time for questions. Her dad approached Jack.

"Hello sir, can I give you a lift home again?"

Jack pulled his coat around him tightly. His tartan pyjamas and slippers were wet and covered in mud. His grey hair was wild and in his eyes was a look of confusion.

"I don't know who you are. No. I need to find my brother. He's coming for my horses and my niece."

"It's okay, Jack, Dad will take you back to Helen," Jessie said gently. She took hold of his hand.

"No," Jack pulled his hand free, "No, I don't know who any of you are."

"Please, Jack. Helen and Anna are waiting for you back at the house. And Luna. He will be wondering where you are."

Jack nodded his head. 'Luna' the word brought with it familiarity.

"Yes. Yes, I need to go back to see Luna."

"Just this way, Jack," Anna's dad put a hand on Jack's shoulder and guided him in the direction of the village and his waiting car.

Chapter 17

They dropped Matthew and Megan off with a neighbour and then drove in silence along the dark lanes up to the Chalkes' farm. Jessie occasionally giving quiet directions to turn left or right from the back seat. She tried to think through the different questions that would soon be fired at her, tried to come up with a good excuse as to why she had behaved the way she had. Why had she lied to everybody around her? Why had she put herself in danger? Why shouldn't she be made to go back to her old home with her dad? She felt sick, not just from the swaying car in the dark, but also from being so nervous that her life would change for the worse.

The dark road and the misty windows with her mum sitting beside her reminded Jessie of the drive down to Cornwall that day, all those weeks ago. Had it really only been a few months? It felt like a lifetime, as though the life she had lived somewhere else was just a dream. She had been so worried about change, but when it happened, it didn't take long to acquire its own routine. A new bed but still the same dread at getting out of its cosy warmth into the coldness of a weekday morning. New dinner plates to eat from but still her mother's terrible cooking piled up on them. A different view out of the window, but still the same thoughts that crept through Jessie's mind each day. Thoughts of family, of friends, of how people felt about her, about what the future was to bring. I wonder if that ever changes, thought Jessie. I wonder if I will think of these things forever?

The car pulled up outside the Chalke's farm. The lights were on in every room and Jessie could see Helen's car parked up outside again. As they got out of the car and neared the house, Jessie could see Helen through the windows, could see the worry on her face and the way she was wringing her hands.

"Jack!" she cried as they entered the house. She kissed him and hugged him tightly. Jack leant into her familiar embrace.

"Come in, come in." Helen ushered Jessie and her parents into the living room. She gently guided Jack into his armchair and called, first the police and then Anna.

"... no, he's fine, love. Home again. Safe and sound. Come over for a while, love. Okay. Yes, okay. See you in a minute."

Helen made tea and brought through five mugs on a tray. They all sat in silence for a moment, sipping at the steaming hot drinks.

"Well, Jess," her dad began "I think you've got some explaining to do."

There was so much that Jessie felt she should say, although she knew what the first word should be. To all of them.

"Sorry," she said quietly, "I'm sorry I lied. I'm sorry I kept secrets from you all. But I only did it because I was scared you'd take me away," she said, looking at her dad, "and scared that you would send me back," she glanced at her mum "and I didn't think you would want me to bother you if you knew," she said to Jack and Helen.

"But it was Luna. Luna was, is, so special to me. I can't imagine not coming here to see him. I can't imagine going away and never seeing him again."

Jessie began to cry and curled up into the sofa cushions like a small child. Her mum put her hand on her arm and rubbed it through the fabric of her jumper.

"Jessie. I know why you did it. But what I don't understand is why you felt the need to put yourself in such danger. If you'd just told me. If you'd just explained..."

"You were too busy," Jessie interrupted, "you were always too busy with Matthew. With Megan. You were sad all the time without Dad."

"Jess, I wasn't," her mum replied, looking nervously across the room to her dad.

"You were Mum!"

"Jessie, calm down," her dad spoke firmly, "don't be rude to your mother."

"What do you care? You have a new life now. You don't care about any of us. You didn't even come down here once all summer!"

"I came the moment I thought there was something wrong though, didn't I?"

"Look," said Jessie's mum "this isn't the time or place. Poor Helen and Jack just want to get to bed, they don't want to be hearing our discussions. Helen, thank you for the tea. And both of you, please, we're so sorry to have caused you all this trouble."

Her mum held Jessie's arm tightly and made her stand up.

"Come on, young lady, time for bed."

At that moment, a cold draft of wintry air blasted through the door and Anna appeared in the hallway. She unwound a green scarf from her neck and hung her coat on the peg. She kicked off her muddy boots and left them on the door mat before coming into the living room. Everybody else was silent as she entered, breathing hard into her hands and rubbing her arms to warm up.

"It's freezing out there," she said, trying to smooth her wild hair. She looked around the room, saw Jessie's red eyes and blotchy face, saw Jessie's parents hard expressions, saw Jack's confusion and Helen's compassion.

"Don't be too hard on her, will you?" she said, gesturing to Jessie, "what she did, it wasn't right, but, she's been a good pal to me these last few weeks."

Anna leant down and squeezed Jessie's shoulder.

"Chin up, kid," she grinned and Jessie smiled shyly back.

Anna walked over to Jack and knelt on the floor in front of him. Jack suddenly leant forward and put both of his hands on Anna's face.

"Uncle Jack. I'm sorry I waited so long to come back. I'm sorry I wasn't here when you needed me, Aunty Helen," she said, taking hold of Jack's hand and looking around to where Helen sat, dabbing at her eyes with a shirt sleeves.

"Come on, Jess," her dad guided her towards the door, "let's get off. Again, everyone, sorry."

They left the cottage. The curtains still had not been drawn, so when Jessie looked back around as they walked down the path, she could see the smile which had lit up Jack's face as Anna leant over and gave him a big hug. Even though Jessie knew that she was in for days of telling off, she felt happy that some good had come of the secrets she had kept.

***

Perhaps that had been the reason for all of it anyway. Perhaps Luna was only ever meant to be a way for Anna to come back into her family's life again. Perhaps it was really Anna who was the one who held Luna's trust. She was his special person, not Jessie after all. The thoughts had been tightly lodged in Jessie's mind for all the following days. At first she felt anger, then sadness and finally acceptance. If this was the way everything was meant to turn out anyway then there was no point in allowing herself to feel anything other than a quiet acceptance.

The days became colder. The Christmas lights had been switched on and every shop was festooned with tinsel and foil decorations hanging in the windows. Gold, green, red, the sparkling colours brought a sense of excitement and anticipation. For mince pies, cakes, presents and Christmas trees were just a few weeks away. The Advent candle which her mum had placed in the living room was only burnt down to the 3rd and on each of those three evenings, with the Christmas tree lights glittering on the tinsel, Jessie's family had gathered around and watched as Mum had cupped her fingers around the match and guided it to the candle wick. The flame glowed softly in the creamy wax and a circle of light was projected onto the wall behind.

With the hot water bottles at night time and porridge in the mornings came a sense of peace that Jessie had always connected with home and family. Before anything else, this familiar comfort had always been there and was what she had missed so much all summer. Her parents were trying harder now to get along. Occasionally they would not be able to stop a barbed comment or irritated expression from crossing their face, but mostly they wrote Christmas cards and went shopping together without any arguments.

"How long are you staying, Dad?" Matthew had asked one evening and their father had just shrugged his shoulders and mumbled a half answer about perhaps for a while, or a while longer anyway.

"But definitely for Christmas!" Matthew had cried.

"Definitely for Christmas."

The end of the school term was nearly in sight and Jessie had barely seen Lauren. Every time they crossed paths in the long corridors, Lauren had quickly looked away. Although, Jessie thought, it no longer seemed that she looked away with anger in her eyes, she seemed nervous, guilty even for allowing their falling out to have lasted so long. They occasionally bumped into each other in the canteen at lunchtime, both girls opening their mouths as though to say something but, neither able to find the words, silently closed them again and scurried past.

Chapter 18

Jessie missed the time she spent with horses and the people she had spent it with. She missed sitting in the tack room with the smell of leather, dust floating in the daylight that streamed through the open door, pressing her fingers to leave prints in the thick, square blocks of orange saddle soap. Cold fingers gripping mugs of hot drinks as the steam warmed the tip of her nose. Just being outside. Being out in the fresh air surrounded by grass and trees and wildlife. It had felt natural to her, the place where she was meant to be.

The short Winter days had meant that Jessie spent more time indoors and she felt like a rabbit in a hutch, a budgie in a cage, a pony in a stable. She needed to be out, to be free, with the wind in her hair and space all around her. Although she no longer had Luna to visit, and she could not tag along with Lauren and Charlie, she suddenly remembered that there were seven other ponies that she had not lost. The wild ponies on the moors. Just because she could not ride or even stroke them didn't mean that she could not learn more about horses just by watching them.

The following Saturday, Jessie waited by her window all morning until she saw Thorn and his herd-mates wander into view. She was prepared. She had all her warmest clothes on and her school rucksack was full with a bottle of juice, some biscuits, an apple and a cheese sandwich. As soon as she spotted the ponies, she dashed downstairs.

"I'll be out in the garden!" she called on her way.

She half walked, half ran down the path. It felt as though the garden were asleep; the daffodils, snowdrops and crocuses were waiting just beneath the soil, ready to burst upwards in bright splashes of colour in the coming weeks. The trees, their naked branches spreading across the grey sky. The bushes and leafy plants covered with frost which had yet to melt as the day had barely warmed up. A noisy crowd of sparrows squabbled over the peanuts in the bird feeder which was swinging wildly.

Jessie dashed up to the end of the garden and sat down on the stone wall. The ponies had ambled along invisible paths, always knowing where they intended to go, and reached the spot outside Jessie's house. This must be a good patch to stop and graze for the herd separated out slightly and seemed less concerned with where the others were. They were all so focused on the grass that they barely seemed to notice Jessie who had taken her sandwich out and started to eat.

Jessie watched the ponies for a couple of hours. Her mum came out and sat with her for a short while before returning to the warmth of the kitchen. Jessie sat, warm and snug in her thermals, and watched. With every minute which passed, with every flick of an ear and wrinkle of nostril, Jessie came to feel that she understood a little more. She noticed the way the ponies behaved, as individuals but also as one part of a whole. There was a deep understanding between each member of the herd, a complex language from pony to pony.

Jessie slid down from the wall, leaving her bag behind. She very slowly made her way over to the ponies. She kept her head down and sidled up to them so that she did not frighten them. The nearest one raised her head and breathed loudly, keeping her dark eyes and pricked ears on Jessie, waiting to decide whether she needed to run. Jessie dropped to the ground and crouched low as she had remembered Jack doing with Luna once before.

She waited, keeping her eyes fixed on the ground until her legs felt tingly with pins and needles. Her patience paid off, however, for she could hear tentative steps coming towards her. She reached out her hand and felt the mare's warm breath on her fingertips, her whiskery muzzle brushed across Jessie's skin and in that one moment of connection, Jessie felt a joy which could not be matched by riding or grooming. She had learnt the pony's language and for one brief moment they had reached out to each other and understood what the other was saying. Whilst riding and jumping and galloping would be fun, it was these moments which, Jessie suddenly understood, were more important.

The spell was broken and Jessie noticed that the herd had moved closer together with Jessie on the edge. All of the ponies were standing with their heads up, staring at something coming from the direction of the sea. Jessie stayed crouched low and tried to see what they were looking at. Gradually, she noticed a shape moving towards them. It was coming at some speed and as it neared Jessie could see that it was another pony.

The wild ponies waited for a moment and one let out soft whicker to the stranger who let out a shrill whinny in reply. However, as the pony neared, Jessie could see that the pony was wearing tack. Stirrups flapped wildly and the reins were trailing dangerously close to the ground. Jessie leapt to her feet, terrified that the pony could put a leg through the looped reins and break it's leg.

Jessie's sudden movement and the sight and sound of the stirrups flapping against the leather saddle made the wild ponies nervous and they turned and moved away in a tight group once more, heading back into the hills. The pony shrieked a loud whinny at their disappearing figures but it was tired and had to slow to a trot. As it came nearer, Jessie recognised the pony. It was Fern. The little skewbald mare that Jessie had ridden all those weeks ago and had raced with Luna across the moors.

Something bad must have happened for Fern to be out here on her own, tacked up but with no rider. Fern had stopped a little distance away and stood, breathing heavily, unsure of what to do next. Jessie walked up to her, murmuring soothing words and hoping that she would just be able to catch hold of the reins before Fern decided to take off again. She reached out and curled her fingers around the rubber reins, breathing a sigh of relief.

"Jessie!" her mum stood on the other side of the wall, her arms full of washing. She had heard the commotion and rushed over.

"We need to get help, Mum."

Jessie's mum dropped the washing on the wall and leapt over.

"Come on."

Jessie ran up the stirrups and loosened Fern's girth. She pulled the reins over Fern's head so that she could lead her properly and they set off. Fern pranced and jogged at first but quickly settled and walked calmly beside Jessie as they made their way across the moors in the direction of the riding stables.

They had only been walking for ten minutes or so before Jessie's mum said,

"Wait a second, listen."

They stopped and stood quietly. At first Jessie thought it was just the sound of the wind or the distant sea but after a few seconds the sound became clearer.

"Help!" a thin voice cried.

Jessie coaxed Fern into a trot and they all ran in the direction of a little rocky gully from where the sound seemed to come.

As they neared, the voice grew clearer and Jessie recognised it instantly.

"Lauren!" she called.

She could just about make out the red and blue silk of Lauren's riding hat and her blonde hair beneath. The path twisted around the hillside and the ground sloped down steeply to a marshy patch of ground onto which Lauren had fallen. She was sitting upright but clutched her arm tightly to her chest.

"Lauren! Are you okay?"

Lauren looked up and saw Jessie, her mum and Fern framed by the rocks and sky.

"Don't worry, sweetheart, just stay nice and still and I'll come and get you," Jessie's mum scrambled down from the path, avoiding the boulders and loose shale until she had reached the bottom. She checked Lauren and asked her questions as Jessie stood up on the path, watching on. Her mum must have decided that Lauren was not too injured as she wrapped an arm around her and helped her to her feet.

"We can't come back up, Jess, we'll have to find a way out from down here. See if you can find a better path for Fern."

They were all reunited a few minutes later and Jessie's mum lifted Lauren onto Fern's back. Lauren was sore and bruised. Her arm was very painful and she had sprained her ankle. Tears stained her cheeks. As Jessie led Fern and Lauren back to the stables, Jessie apologised for everything and by the time they had reached the yard all was forgotten and they were friends once more.

***

As chaos descended on the riding school with people dashing around calling ambulances, taking Fern back into the stables and asking Lauren a hundred questions, Jessie and her mum sat quietly on a mounting block together.

"I'm so proud of you, Jess; of how you apologised to Lauren and how you handled Fern. You're quite the horsewoman now, when did that happen, eh?" she asked.

Jessie shrugged her shoulders.

"You're a natural," she continued "I only wish we had the money so that we could afford for you to have riding lessons, or a pony on loan or something. But, I'm sure, one day, you will be able to have horses in your life. If you want something enough, and are prepared to work hard enough and maybe to give up other things."

"I want it more than anything. I'm prepared to do anything," Jessie looked at the ponies on the yard and wondered if their owners realised just how lucky they were. Whether they appreciated the gift that had been given to them in the time they had to spend with their horses each day.

"Well, then, it'll happen."

Chapter 19

"It's the holidays!" A blur of blonde hair and a tight one-armed hug wrapped tightly around Jessie the moment she opened the door. Lauren stood on the doorstep grinning. One arm was strapped up in a sling, the other hand held her riding helmet and happiness sparkled in her eyes.

"I'm glad we're friends again," she said as she kicked Jessie's trainers in her direction and grabbed her coat off the hook, "I was so bored riding by myself. We've got the whole holidays to go riding together."

"I haven't got a horse," Jessie said, glumly.

"You can ride one of the riding school ponies. They don't get ridden so much in the winter, Jane will be happy you can give one some exercise."

"I don't know," Jessie said. She felt as though something had changed now. Since meeting Anna and spending time with the moorland ponies, she had started to question everything. There was something about the way those riding school ponies were handled, kept and ridden that made Jessie feel uncomfortable.

"Come on," Lauren whined, "it'll be fun." She shoved Jessie's coat in her hand.

"Maybe."

"We could ride across to the tor and see how Luna is doing."

That was enough to encourage Jessie to put her trainers on and pick up her riding helmet that was on the side. She told her parents where she was going and, then, was off, racing down the path behind Lauren. They ran on, down the lane, through the gate, across the moors until they were tired and could barely speak for trying to catch their breath.

When they got to the yard, Jane, the yard manager, quickly found a hairy, muddy pony for Jessie to groom. The dust made her cough as she tackled the mud with a rubber curry comb but eventually made him look presentable enough to tack up. Lauren sat on Charlie in the yard, waiting for Jessie. She lolled in the saddle, her feet out of the stirrups and arms by her sides. She was more confident riding the safe, dependable Charlie than the flighty Fern.

"Come onnnnnn!" she whined.

They rode across the moors as they had so many times the previous summer. Only this time, instead of t-shirts and rucksacks full of cold drinks, they were bundled up in layers of clothing and tights under their jodhpurs.

The air was still and smelt fresh and metallic. The grey clouds threatened rain as the two girls rode on towards the Chalke's farm. They veered upwards. Across the browns and oranges of the wintry grass and heather. The gorse had only a few scattered yellow flowers, rather than the thick clusters of coconut scented petals of summertime. Gulls circled in the sky and jackdaws chattered as they flew around the headland in a flock. The rugged cliffs and the sea just beyond were dark and dramatic and for a moment,

Jessie felt like she could be living in any age, at any time. She expected to see a pirate ship's black flags appear over the horizon or a flash of a mermaid's tail as she swam down, down, down into the murky green depths.

"I love this place so much," she breathed.

"What?" Lauren shouted.

As they climbed a little higher, the land stretched out far below all the way to the sea. There was Luna. A white shape in the field. He grazed with Bob by his side, just a short distance between them and Jessie thought of the moorland ponies who often seemed to be grazing on the same patch of grass even though they had a whole moor-full.

"There he is!" Lauren grinned, pointing at Luna. He surely could not have seen them all this distance away, but at that moment he lifted his head and looked in their direction. A wave of sadness flooded through Jessie as she remembered a time when he had looked at her and whinnied a greeting.

She noticed a person standing beside the gate. She could not make out whether it was Anna, Helen or Jack as the person was too far away. But the person had spotted them and waved their arms backwards and forwards. Lauren waved back but Jessie sat still. Her throat felt tight and she tried to bite her lip to hold back the tears.

"We should go down and say hello," Lauren suggested.

"No! We mustn't. Come on, let's head back."

Jessie picked up her reins, squeezed with her legs and clicked with her tongue to encourage her pony into a trot and both girls continued to follow the track over the brow of the hill. They spotted the herd of ponies who were heading in the direction of the lake and the hut and so they followed them. Charlie and Jessie's pony, Robin, pricked their ears and walked a little quicker as the ponies drew near.

"It's been ages since we've been up here."

"Not so long for me," Jessie cringed with the memory of the darkness and Jack, lost, up here just a short time ago.

"Oh yeah, sorry."

Jessie peered into the hut and saw that there was even more things in there now. Pots and pans. Mugs. An old metal kettle. Jars and containers of sugar and cracker biscuits and porridge oats. There was a tatty arm chair and a newspaper. Photographs. A few blankets and a thick, winter coat.

"Someone's been busy."

Jessie could imagine Anna sitting in here, staring out at the lake and eating crackers. The crumbs falling to the floor for seagulls brave enough to venture inside. The sun setting and blue shadows creeping across the ground. Although the hut had been Lauren and Jessie's secret camp, it felt, now, like it was someone else's. Just as Luna no longer felt like he could ever be hers, neither could this place.

Jessie felt strangely homesick. Although this hut was nothing like a real home, there was something that made Jessie miss having a place that was hers. That she could go back to. She thought of Rose Cottage, did that feel like home anymore? With her dad's suitcase overflowing in the corner of the living room and his sleeping bag hastily rolled up each morning, it felt temporary. As though things were likely to change, yet again, at any moment.

A few days later, after the advent candle had been burnt down to number 17, Jessie lay in bed and came to a sudden realisation. She got out of bed, put on her dressing gown and crept downstairs. Her parents were still up, she could see the light shining under the door and hear voices on the television. She pushed the door open slowly, the scent of the Christmas tree was warm and comforting as Jessie poked her head around the doorframe.

"What are you doing up?" her mum asked, looking up from the film that her parents had been watching.

"Couldn't sleep. Can I ask you something?"

"Of course."

"Dad, when you go back after Christmas, can I come with you?"

This time, Jessie really *did* mean it. She knew that she wouldn't change her mind and even though her mum had looked devastated and her dad hadn't known what to say to her, Jessie thought that it would be for the best.

"You told me just a few days ago that you wanted to be around horses," her mum cried, "you said that you were prepared to work hard, to do whatever it takes. I didn't expect you to give up quite so easily, Jess."

"But that was before I realised that it was impossible. It's a dream for other people, not for me," Jessie snapped and dashed back upstairs and curled into her bed.

***

Neither of her parents mentioned anything about that night again in the following days. Jessie, however, was counting down the time. She counted down all of the 'last times' - the last visit to the hut, the last trip into town, the last time she'd have her hair cut by Mary in the village. Every last time made Jessie dread those that were still to come. The last time she would see the moorland ponies, the last time she would see Lauren. Perhaps some last times had already slipped by without her realising; the last time she'd go to the hut, the last time she'd see Jack and Helen and Anna. The last time she'd see Luna.

Jessie realised with a start. The last time she'd see Luna. It had been and gone. What possible reason could she have to go and visit him one more time. That last memory of him as a distant white shape in the field would be her final memory. The thought of it made her want to cry.

At least she would make sure her last day with Lauren would be a good one. Jessie had not told

Lauren anything, but two days before Christmas they arranged to meet up, dress Charlie in tinsel and take him down to the beach.

It was still early in the morning when they tacked Charlie up and Lauren mounted from the mounting block. Jessie walked behind in silence as they made their way through the little woodland, down the street where cats lounged on cushions behind misty windows, along the edge of the field and down the stony track which, finally, led out onto the huge expanse of beach.

"Come on!" Jessie ran ahead, the breeze in her hair. Despite the cold, she kicked her shoes off and ran barefoot down towards the sea. Lauren held Charlie back for a moment, waiting for Jessie to turn around and look back before letting him gallop towards her - mane flying wildly and sand spraying up behind him. She pulled him up before reaching Jessie and the pair started laughing madly.

They walked along the shoreline, chatting and giggling, and Jessie could not bring herself to tell Lauren that this would be the last time they would see each other. Maybe I won't say anything, Jessie thought, better to just sneak off quietly and still keep this one good memory rather than ruin it.

As they were starting to head back up the beach, Jessie was reminded of that summer day when this place was so new to her. An elderly couple, arm in arm, came out of the cafe and climbed slowly down the steps onto the sand. The man was tall and thin, dressed smartly and the lady had a string of red beads around her neck. It was Helen and Jack. Only, unlike before, just a few steps behind them was Anna. She was chatting to the waiter as she closed the door and tugged her coat tightly around her, pulling her red hair free of the collar to dance in the breeze.

"Come on. Let's go."

If Jessie had not been in such a hurry to avoid the Chalkes, she might have noticed somebody else in the cafe. Her mum sat in the window, finishing the last of her coffee, her mind deep in thought. She had watched her daughter running barefoot across the sand, laughing and joking with her friend, and she knew that she had made the right decision in contacting Helen. A few moments after Anna, Helen and Jack left, so too, did Jessie's mum, walking down the same steps and following Charlie's hoof prints back up the path.

Chapter 20

Christmas morning. Jessie was woken up by cold hands tapping her face, tugging her hair and finally, when she opened her eyes, she saw her brother's face inches away from her own.

"Wake up, lazy, it's Christmas!" he grinned, pulling his stocking onto her bed and climbing under the covers at the other end from Jessie. They poked and prodded at the pile of presents, trying to guess what they were. Pulling the paper away from the corners and trying to look inside without ripping the shiny, colourful wrapping paper.

The morning passed by slowly, mostly spent waiting until they could open their presents, which, when the time finally arrived, was over in a flash leaving the living room strewn in paper and ribbon. Jessie was mostly distracted from any other thoughts by the excitement, but now that it was over and she was sitting on the sofa alone, waiting for her turn in the shower, she looked out of the window and her thoughts turned once more to the day she would leave this place forever.

Beyond the window, the garden was covered in a thick frost. The sky was watery blue with a few grey clouds that moved by slowly. A scattering of early daffodils had started to poke their yellow heads above the earth and the brightness of them seemed so out of place amongst the sleepy foliage.

"Shower's free, Jess!" the shout came down the stairs, and as Jessie headed into the steamy bathroom, she made a decision to enjoy these last moments of her family being together for she knew that they would soon be over.

Jessie got dressed, brushed her hair and cleaned her teeth. It took her some time before she realised that the house had gone very quiet. Strange, she thought, surely there should be the sound of Matthew laughing as he rugby tackled their dad, a ball of limbs as they wrestled amongst the scraps of glittery wrapping paper. Surely there should be the smell of turkey cooking in the oven and the clatter of cutlery and plates coming from the kitchen. Yet there was nothing except silence and a strange feeling that she was alone in the house.

Jessie crept downstairs, the silence making her want to be quiet herself.

"Hello?" she said, peering around the door.

Anna sat in the armchair.

"You know," she said "you do take a long time to get yourself ready. Come on. They asked me to come and get you."

Jessie was confused.

"Who did?"

"Everyone. Come on. Get your coat. Oh, and, here... present from me."

Anna passed Jessie a box wrapped in shiny gold paper. Jessie held it and looked up at Anna.

"Well, open it then!"

Inside the box was a riding helmet. It was brand new and the soft cushioning inside was thick and fresh. Nothing like the tatty, smelly hats which she had been borrowing from the riding school.

"Thanks, only, I don't need it anymore."

"Course you do," she said, ushering Jessie to the door, "don't you go thinking that you'll be riding him without one."

Anna flung open the door and there, standing amongst the daffodils, was Luna. He lifted his head and pricked his ears and whickered the same soft greeting that had made Jessie's heart melt that day back in the summer. His white coat was thick and woolly but it gleamed under the winter sunshine. His dark eyes were bright and his mane and tail looked soft and brushed. He wore a clean brown leather saddle and his bridle was polished and shiny.

"I can't, I can't!" Jessie sobbed, "I can't ride him and know that it will be the last time."

"It's the first time," Anna soothed.

"The first and the last. Please. I'll be going away in a few days."

"Come on. Everyone's waiting," Anna said, "you're not the only one any good at keeping secrets."

Jessie wiped her eyes and walked up to Luna. She reached out and felt his whiskery muzzle breathe warm air on her cold fingertips. She leaned forward and kissed his soft nose. Anna adjusted the stirrups and girth and gave Jessie a leg up into the saddle. She felt higher up than she had on Charlie or Fern, yet Luna was older and wiser than those ponies and Jessie instantly felt safe on his back.

She sat up straight and tall, making sure her position was as perfect as she could. Held the reins in the proper way and, with a gentle squeeze, they were off. Anna walked alongside as they made their way down the road towards the beach.

With the smell of the sea in the air and the sound of the waves and gulls as they circled in the pale blue sky, Anna and Jessie walked and chatted. They passed a few people in the street and Jessie felt very proud to be riding such a beautiful horse as Luna.

"Merry Christmas!" they called as they passed.

Inside the houses, children peered out from the glow of Christmas tree lights and decorations. Still in their pyjamas they clutched their new toys and waved as Jessie rode past the window.

On the edge of the beach, at the top of the dunes where the path wound down to the open expanse of sand, Jessie saw a rucksack tucked amongst a patch of long marram grass.

"This is where I leave you," Anna said, stopping and picking up the rucksack.

Panic and dread lurched in the pit of Jessie's stomach.

"What? No!" she cried, "you need to stay. To look after Luna when I go away. You can't leave!"

Anna smiled.

"I need to go."

"No, please. What more could you possibly want? You have everything. You are so lucky. What else is there?"

"I am very lucky. And it was you who helped me see that. But, I was never much good at staying in one place."

"But Luna..."

"Luna will be just fine. He'll be in very good hands," she said with a knowing smile.

Jessie leant down as far as she could without falling off and wrapped her arms around Anna's neck.

"Bye," she said, quietly.

"Goodbye," Anna replied, "now, you take this old boy down to the beach. Everyone's waiting for you by the cafe."

Jessie felt a little nervous as she squeezed her legs and Luna moved off, down the dunes, along the path avoiding the hawthorn and thick patches of spiky marram grass. Luna walked quickly but he was sure footed as he marched down the hill and out onto the firm sand of the beach below.

Jessie turned to see the cafe at the far end of the beach. She could see her family waiting outside. Jack and Helen were there too and Lauren was holding Bob, the rest of her family standing to her side. Jessie turned to look back up the dunes. Anna stood at the top, framed by the sky and clouds, her red hair streaming out behind her. She pulled her rucksack onto her back and waved her arms wide.

"Take good care of him!" she shouted, her voice thin and weak above the cries of the gulls. And Jessie suddenly realised. She wouldn't be the one moving away. She would be staying right here, with Luna to look after, their adventures together only just beginning.

She leant down and scratched his withers.

"Come on then, boy," she murmured, picking up the loose reins and asking Luna to trot.

Trot quickly became canter as Luna's hooves thundered through the wet sand. Jessie felt her heart quicken. She stood up a little, crouching over his neck and she could feel his mane brushing against her fingers. The creak of the leather tack, the sound of Luna's breathing, the feel of his sides against her legs. It was as though time stopped for a moment. It was like being inside a photograph, the gulls hung in mid air, the droplets of sea spray catching the light and forming rainbows. The shapes of her family and friends standing to one side, watching.

Luna slowed to a trot as he neared them and Jessie tipped her head to the sky, feeling the cold air on her hot skin. She flopped down and wrapped her arms around his neck as Luna stood on the sand, blowing hard, sides heaving. Lauren ran across the sand with Bob trotting beside her, his little legs moving so fast they were almost a blur.

"He's yours to have on loan, Jess," the words tumbled from Lauren's mouth as Jessie slid down from Luna's back and clutched the reins tightly.

~ 179 ~

She looked back up the dunes and could just about see the dark shape which was Anna walking along the coast path. Her rucksack heavy on her back and with no plans of where her journey would take her next. She thought of her dad's suitcase waiting beside the stairs back at home. He, too, would be leaving soon. Changes, new starts and different experiences would always be just around the corner, yet, with Luna waiting for her every evening. Standing behind the gate, whickering at her as she prepared his feed and haynet, Jessie thought she could cope with anything else which life threw at her.

37369716R00107

Printed in Great Britain
by Amazon